THE GREENLYS

HISTORICAL EYEWITNESSES

1415 – 1865

David Greenly

Copyright © 2023 David Greenly

All rights reserved.

ISBN: **9798393761882**

CONTENTS

INTRODUCTION	1
PART ONE: THE COUNTY OF HEREFORDSHIRE, ENGLAND (1830)	4
PART TWO: THE PREPARATIONS	13
PART THREE: THE ARRIVAL	19
PART FOUR: LUMBERMAN, FARMER, AND WAR	25
PART FIVE: DISEASE AND DEATH	29
PART SIX: HENRY V (1415) & WILLIAM SHAKESPEARE (1600)	38
PART SEVEN: THE AMERICAN CIVIL WAR (1861 – 1865)	43
PART EIGHT: JOHN GREENLY & THE BATTLE OF TRAFALGAR (1805)	47
PART NINE: SALISBURY CATHEDRAL & JOHN CONSTABLE	61
PART TEN: LADY ELIZABETH GREENLY, REGENCY DIARIST (1771 – 1839)	63

INTRODUCTION

This book tells an historical story, a story which is spread over hundreds of years, from 1415 to 1865, and covers from that period, some of the most important historical events, and characters, in both English and American history.

Intriguingly, the story is based on eyewitness accounts from members of a single long time established English family, called the Greenlys. Or more correctly, this book tells a partial story, as it concerns just a few members of that family, who, on the face of it, share nothing much in common, other than the fact that these relatives all lived within a few miles of each other, around two hundred years ago, in the northwest corner of an English county called Herefordshire.

The story that is told here, is only possible because the family tree for the Greenlys, has very long and deep roots. These roots, and just as for everyone else's families too, reach back in time through countless thousands of years of human history. And just as it is for all families, there will be a point in that long lineage, that is much closer to the current time, where a family can build their own history forward from. That point in time, may be as recently as a generation ago or even a thousand years in the past, or at any date in between.

The Greenly family have a traceable lineage, which stretches back as far as 850AD, to the ancient times of King Alfred the Great, who in those far off days ruled the northern parts of an island that we now call England. Only two hundred years earlier, the legends of King Arthur and the Knights of The Roundtable, and the mystical Merlin were born and passed forever into English folklore. Those times are regarded as the formative years of the history of England.

THE GREENLYS: HISTORICAL EYEWITNESSES 1415 - 1865

Since those ancient days, and as is the case for all families, the Greenlys have branched out. Some branches stayed in the same location for generations, and others reached out further, either through choice, or sometimes through necessity. And all of the many blood lines, that flow along those branches, of course, made their own history. That history, or parts of it at least, was passed on through records, such as parish or court documents. But most family history was passed on through the generations by word of mouth or handed down as stories or written up more formally in the family bibles and personal diaries, when, and if they were kept, and survived. Occasionally, a family may have been significant enough to have their portraits painted. These portraits can provide an interesting source of reference, as some physical features may pass down through the generations.

For the past twenty five years, the author has researched the Greenly family history. The relative novelty of the family name, and its traceability through the inevitable spelling variations over the ages, and the fact that good parts of the history are available in public and private archives, has helped greatly.

Increasingly, with the digitisation of numerous documentation sources and official records, coupled with the easy access to powerful genealogy tools for building and searching family trees, it is possible to add provenance to stories.

The relatively recent ability to validate family trees via DNA, can now enable indisputable evidence of a family connection to ancestral events and people.

The author's research has revealed ancestors who were present at major historical events, and ancestors who had walked alongside the great and good. However, most of the history would involve generations going about their daily family lives, in what they probably saw at the time as a mundane passage, with the normal life events; the births, and the deaths and the marriages – providing the breaks in the daily ebb and flow of things. But as we will see on these pages, all family history is interesting, even if it does not feel so at that time.

This book tells the historical story of a select few of the Greenly family living around the end of the 18th and into the 19th Century. In addition, there are also some significant family stories shared from before those dates.

THE GREENLYS: HISTORICAL EYEWITNESSES 1415 - 1865

An ancestor of the author, born in the late 18th century, has been chosen to act as a reference point, to whom all of the threads of the characters, and their stories told on these pages, can be tied back to. It is a fascinating curiosity, that today, we can know more of a person and their own intertwine with history, than they could ever have imagined for themselves, even in their wildest dreams.

This book is structured around a main character called Richard Greenly, who is a bloodline ancestor of the author. Richard was born in 1787. Richard lived for many years around the same area of North Herefordshire, as had generations of his Greenly relatives before him. Richard's own story, and how his family story intertwined with that of his cousins – both those who were close and those that were distant – and also how it intertwined with his distant ancestors own stories too, is told in a way that I hope, transports you back to the times, and the places and the lives of those that were present at the events described. I hope that you might develop a sense for a specific individual and share their life for a short while.

There are good times, and there are bad times. There are happy times, and there are sad times. There are heroic times, and there are tragic times. All life is shared here.

This account is based on real characters, who were eyewitnesses at some of the most defining historical events, in both English and American history.

David Greenly hereby asserts his right to be identified as the creator of this book.
© David Greenly 2023

PART ONE

THE COUNTY OF HEREFORDSHIRE, ENGLAND
(1830)

The once so reliable climate of England, with its four distinct seasons, had been thrown into turmoil. In April 1815, England was enjoying the usual Spring warmth, but on the other side of the world, a volcano named Tambora, erupted so massively that it would disrupt weather patterns over England for years to come. Winters were so severe, that the river Thames froze over for weeks at a time, and Londoners would skate on it, and enjoy the frost-fairs, held on its frozen surface. The spring and summers were at once hellishly hot, or the sky was dark and heavy with cloud, that could soak the earth for weeks on-end, with pulverising rain that would cause the precious few inches of top soil – that was nurtured by the farmers over many generations - to be washed away into the ditches surrounding the fields and then, with the water ever seeking the lowest point of the land, the soil would trickle as a sludge to the brooks that themselves flowed into the larger rivers and the soil would be lost forever.

Farmers all over England looked skywards. They prayed in their churches, and they prayed in their homes. Harvests were exceptionally poor. Soil and crop disease, led to corn and potato famines. The potato famine was especially severe in Ireland. Thousands of starving Irish crossed the Irish Sea and came to England, via Wales, and walked through

Herefordshire, on their way to the bigger towns and cities, praying that they would find work and food. And when their praying deserted them, they stole and they begged, and they died in their hundreds, in the fields and by the roadsides. They found no relief in England. All they found was countryside folk just like themselves; struggling, scared and increasingly desperate too.

Because of the failing harvests, the price of flour was now beyond the reach of most, and even the pampered rich could not easily find supplies of it. The rich in society had, for many years, used flour to liberally powder their faces and wigs as was the fashion of the higher ranks in society at that time. Wearing wigs eventually fell out of fashion as a result. Nonetheless, the government, looking to raise funds from the crisis, introduced a tax for purchasing flour for wigs, and in Bristol, for example, over two thousand licences were granted at one guinea per head. The poor of England, appalled at this vain behaviour, while many around were starving, called the wig wearers - 'guinea pigs'. England was on the brink of an economic disaster. And some feared that the poor could even rise up in revolution, as was happening in other parts of Europe. This was not just an idle worry, as all knew that there had been 'peasant revolts' in England in former times.

And it was not just the farming crisis that fuelled this economic and political tension. Thousands of British soldiers, who were returning home from fighting in the Napoleonic wars in France, after the defeat of Napoleon at The Battle of Waterloo in 1814, could not find work. Additionally, a new invention put thousands more out of jobs. The invention was a new farming machine, which could thresh corn, to separate the seeds from the stalks, without the need for the men's manual labour; labour that they and their families had provided for generations, at each harvest time. Many poor farm workers rioted across the whole country, and smashed the machines, and attacked the farm owners. Many wondered how they and their family would survive another harsh winter.

Local parish authorities were trying their best to feed the starving but knew that something radical had to be done. There were simply too many starving and destitute people, and not enough food to sustain them. Some parishes provided funding for apprenticeships – where some young people from the parish could learn a trade over seven years, and hopefully, use that trade to provide their future. A few apprenticeships were local to the parish, but most were in the larger towns and cities, meaning the young people would have to leave home. Fourteen years old was the typical age to start the apprenticeship.

Richard Greenly sat quietly with his wife Hannah, and their seven children, in their plain but comfortable oak framed farmhouse. Richard had built his home with his father John, in a quiet hamlet, called Eardisland, in the rich rolling pastures of a northeast corner of Herefordshire, in England. Eardisland was nestled alongside the border with Wales. The land between Eardisland and Wales, was sometimes called 'no-man's land'. Richard quietly folded his newspaper. He held it in his strong worn hands, hands that were hewn from years of farming and woodworking, just as generations of his family had done since medieval times, around this same area. Richard did not usually bother with newspapers. He would get his news from the local clergy, and friends and neighbours, or sometimes from someone returning from a larger town or city. But someone, on returning from a visit to the city of Hereford, had given him a newspaper and had told Richard that the paper mentioned news of a young cousin. The young cousin that was mentioned was Edward Greenly.

A few lines in the newspaper reported on his tragic drowning, while he was swimming in the river Wye, which ran through the city of Hereford. 'Edward was an inexperienced swimmer and had sadly got out of his depth', the report said. Young Edward died aged just fifteen years old. He was the son of Edward Greenly senior. Edward senior, and a brother called John Greenly, had moved to the city of Hereford, from Staunton-on-Arrow years earlier, in order to re-establish a business making gloves. Another brother, William, was also in the city of Hereford at that time and traded as a Crop Merchant and Victualler. Greenlys had been established as Glovemakers in Hereford since the 16th century, and the wearing of gloves was again in the ascendency, having been depressed for a few years before Edward and John went to Hereford to revitalise the family's business there.

William was the father of the Reverend John Greenly. William was prospering as a merchant and lived in 'The Saracens Head Tavern', which was the first dwelling house that you came across within the city walls, after travelling over a medieval stone bridge which was supported by five arches, and which spanned the river Wye. The tavern had gardens, which ran down a slope to the river's edge, and barges would moor alongside on completion of their journey, bringing goods up from the large port city of Bristol, which was located on the southwest coast of England. William was prosperous enough to be able to send his son John, to Oxford University, to study Theology at Christ Church college.

John graduated from Oxford University in 1800, and after a short while spent back at home with his father in Hereford, he joined the Royal Navy as a Chaplain. Reverend John's first ship was called the 'Revenge'. John joined the Revenge when she was newly built in the Spring of 1805.

Revenge was a new design of warship and was easy to manoeuvre in the water. In late October of that same year, John would serve alongside Admiral Lord Nelson, at The Battle of Trafalgar, where Nelson defeated the combined force of Napoleon Bonaparte's French and Spanish fleets.

Richard solemnly read the news report of poor Edward. He wondered if Edward had gone to clean himself in the river, as his work as a glover was a dirty one, especially if he was cleaning and preparing the skins. It was common for workers to bathe in the river, especially during the warmer months.

But it was an advertisement on the same page as Edwards report, that he had happened to notice. The advertisement had captured him. He did not bother with the remainder of the news in the paper, but rather he read the small advertisement, over and over again.
Based on that advertisement, Richard was about to make a monumental decision. Just like the soil that he had ploughed for years and years, he'd been turning this decision over and over in his mind. He turned it over while he walked the fields, and he turned it over while he sat in the evening with his family, and he even turned it over in his dreams. This was the biggest decision he would ever have to make, and it would impact his own family for generations to come.

Richard let out a long and weary sigh. His mind flew wildly about, just as the parched soil did on his farm, and all the farms around here, and all the farms across the country. The drought and crop failures had already ruined many families, as their strips of land, and garden orchards, could no longer produce enough for them all, as they had done, for many generations that had come before.

Many children of these proud families had already left the countryside, and had travelled to the cities, looking for a brighter future, or any future come to that. Some would find work as servants, or labourers, and a few lucky ones would be taken on an apprenticeship, to learn a trade over seven years. Many others struggled however, and fell into the petty crime wave, that this influx of countryside immigrants had caused.

These were hard times. People were becoming increasingly desperate. And desperate people, do desperate things. Richard's brother told him of a cousin's son, young Henry, who was sentenced to death aged twenty-one years old, for breaking into a house in London and stealing clothes. This poor lad was not hanged, as the sentence was changed. Instead of hanging, he was transported to the penal colony of Tasmania. He was to serve 14 years for his crime. Henry served his time, and he managed to return to England, but died a pauper in old age. Richard knew Henry. He knew him while he was growing up, and Richard knew that he was a good boy. Richard, also heard of another cousin, young Elizabeth. Elizabeth was aged twenty years old, and she was sentenced for being a vagrant, in Cheltenham, Gloucestershire.

Richard knew that if he stayed, and did nothing, that his own beloved family could also be torn apart. He simply could not bear the thought. His stomach churned, as he thought of those young people ending up in such dire straits. He could not bear to think of Henry being chained, and thrown into the bowels of a prison ship, for the five months it would take to arrive in Tasmania. Richard screwed his eyes tightly, and he shook his head, to clear the haunting thoughts.

Richard lifted up his paper and read once again. He started at that same page, and eventually his eyes left the advertisement, and stared off into the distance. He was looking blankly out of the window, at his own farmyard, with his tools scattered in every corner, and beyond the yard he looked out to his few acres of land, that he knew so very well. For many years he had seen the barley and the wheat beginning to spring up, and sway in a gentle spring breeze. He would see his little vegetable plot, which was just beside the kitchen door, where he would raise sweet smelling herbs and strawberries, and watch the summer bees dancing over them. He would stand in the gentle and warm summer rain, and watch as it soaked into his soil. He had felt blessed. All that he and his family needed, he could provide, and more. After a while, he blinked his eyes a few times, and turned his gaze and attention back to his family and calmly, almost resignedly, asked his oldest son, also called Richard, to find his father and his brothers, who all lived locally, and he was to ask them to come to his home that evening, to discuss Richard's decision.

That evening, all the Greenly family had gathered, the men, the women, and the children of all the ages. Despite it being the evening, it was still stiflingly hot. The family all sat around Richard, with some by the open doors and windows for air. Some of the younger children were outside playing with the animals. Richard was standing by the cabinet that held the families best pewter plates and mugs, and looked at all the family gathered, and he smiled a gentle, but strong smile. He was finding an inner strength from somewhere.

Richard started to speak. "I'm glad that our grandfather John is not alive to hear what I have to say". His grandfather John had died the year before, and who, only a few years earlier, had sold an impressive farmhouse, and one hundred acres of prime farming land, just up the country lane from where they were all gathered.

Death had come three times in the past year for the Greenlys, and had taken old grandfather John, who died in his sleep, and, it had also taken Richard and Hannah's little daughter, called Hannah after her mother, when she was just two years old, and finally it took their son, Thomas, who had just turned thirteen years old. It was the red fever that took those two.
Richard looked back further from those dreadful times, and thought about the more prosperous and happy times, and then he spoke. "In this paper there is an advertisement". Richard held up the folded Hereford Times and pointed at the advertisement. Some of those sat closest could see that it showed a crude block cut print of a three-mast sailing ship. Not that any of them had ever seen one, other than in their schoolbooks, when they had been taught all about the Vikings, and also about the 'Pilgrim Fathers,' who had sailed from England to America, aboard the Mayflower.

Richard continued. "There is an advertisement here, calling for families with farming and husbandry skills, to come to America, where the land is cheap, and work is well paid and plentiful, and a good and prosperous future can be had for those who worked hard". He paused. "Ships sail bound for America from the Liverpool port in the north each Wednesday". He paused again, hardly believing what he was about to say. He looked to his wife who smiled reassuringly back. They had discussed this decision many times in the past, and Hannah said they should trust in God, as they always had, and reminded her husband that her own distant relative, William Bradford, had been one of the founding fathers of America, and were known as the 'pilgrims'. Richard's father John, put his own tired hand on his son's arm, and everyone there assembled held their breath, waiting to hear what Richard was to say next. "Hannah and I, and the children, are going to start a new life in America". Richard paused to make sure that he had been heard. "In a place called the state of Pennsylvania, which is on the eastern coast of America.," he added.

Richard sold his farmhouse and gifted his land to his brothers. Then, together with his father and brothers, they carefully loaded his tools and a few precious family possessions into a large waggon. The waggon had two huge wheels and was drawn by a large young mare. Richard had built the waggon and had made most of his own farming tools. He could work with wood and iron as competently as any man. His family were also skilled in finding water and sank wells on farms all over Herefordshire. They built and installed the wind pumps, to raise the water, and irrigate the fields. It was known thereabouts, that a Greenly could walk a field, with a birch twitch held in his hands, and with that twitch he could find water beneath the soil. One Greenly had left his farming and had moved to London and was prospering by finding water for the brewery companies, who were springing up all over, and needed a ready supply. A London newspaper had said, 'he could find water where many others had failed'.

Hannah and the younger children would ride on the cart, and Richard and his older sons, who were nearing adulthood, would walk alongside. The journey north to Liverpool would take three days of walking to cover the one hundred miles. The family would sleep under the stars on the way. They loaded enough food for the journey and said their goodbyes. Goodbye to hundreds of years spent on these lands. Goodbye to family and friends that they may never see again.

Richard gave a gentle pull on the bridle, and the horse moved forward, and the waggon jerked, and then moved forward too. Hannah and the children cried. The family that was left behind cried. Some of those left behind would travel alongside the waggon, for as long as they could. Richard never looked back. He could not bring himself to do so. He hid his own tears from his sons, but he could not hide them from Hannah.

Finally, they arrived in Liverpool. The journey had taken longer than expected as some of the roads were in poor repair. Having no further need for the horse and waggon, Richard sold them for twenty one pounds. The family then had to find temporary accommodation. They needed somewhere to stay until the ship was ready to set sail. The Liverpool corporation was struggling to cope with the numbers of English emigrants, who were now joined by Scottish and Irish emigrants too, fleeing famine in Ireland and land clearances in Scotland.

It was common for local Liverpool gangs, to raid a dwelling and demand money or goods from the families, as they knew they would be holding considerable amounts. Richard and his sons were strong. They had tools by their sides. No one came to trouble them.

During the days of their wait, while the ship was being made ready, the family would walk around the docks. They would take in the sights and sounds of the many ships being loaded and unloaded. They would see the huge sacks of cotton that arrived from America. They would watch as the sacks were loaded by the dock hands straight onto the carriages of the new steam trains, which had started to run on the just opened Liverpool to Manchester railway. The cotton was being taken to the factories of the north and were driving the start of England's great Industrial Revolution.

They would pass swiftly by the boisterous taverns on the waterfront, with its open faces and accents that they had never seen or heard before. Richard was aware that some would laugh at him and his families clothing which clearly showed that they had travelled in from the countryside. Richard thought to himself that this was a strange thing to be only one hundred miles distance from the familiarity of home and find people behaving unkindly just because they looked different.

They saw a fine stagecoach, painted in yellow and green. On a board alongside the stagecoach, it advertised that this was a 'Greenly Stagecoach,' and that it was bound for a comfortable and rapid passage to London. The board included the prices for travelling inside the coach, or 'up top,' with the driver and the guard. The boards also included the leaving time from Liverpool and the arrival time in London. It also advised where they would make the overnight stops, at various staging posts. At these places, the passengers would sleep and eat in an Inn, and the horses would be fed and rested, or changed. The coachmen and their passengers had to be cautious at these stops, as it was common for an Inn keeper or others, to pass on information, about the passengers and their luggage, to the notorious footpads and highway men who may wait up the road in order to hold them up.

Richard did not meet the Greenly who advertised the service, but a coachman said that they ran a service each Wednesday.

Soon the ship was ready to sail. Richard and his family stood on the deck of their ship, and looked up at the three large masts, and each with their vast sails. They felt the ship groan as the wind took hold, and they were underway. Many on board had relatives and friends on the dockside to wave them off. They all looked back towards Liverpool, and at England getting smaller and smaller. Then they looked forward and across to the horizon, where eventually they would hear a cry of 'land ahoy,' from a lookout sitting high up in the mast in the 'crows' nest.' Then, the American port of Philadelphia in Pennsylvania, would appear and the journey would be at an end. Or rather, it would just be beginning.

The journey would take thirty-five days, but possibly longer depending on the weather. Sea sickness, and disease bought on board, was a common scourge. Disease would spread quickly in the cramped conditions. A number of passengers would succumb and die. Sadly, those who died had to be buried at sea. Richard thought of the lovely churchyard in Staunton-on-Arrow, and how all his ancestors and near family could be visited there. He thought it must be very hard, to see a loved one slip beneath the waves, and with no permanent place for them to be remembered.

By good fortune, and following a harsh passage, Richard, Hannah and their seven children all arrived safely, and no doubt they were grateful to be off the rolling ship, and onto firmer footings.

PART TWO

THE PREPARATIONS

During the weeks, between the decision and the departure, there was much to be done. Since the decision, Richard, and Hannah, had slowly begun to feel more and more a sense of excitement, at the possibility of their new start in far off America, and the gnawing feeling of apprehension – of leaving their loved ones and leaving them at this desperate time, and leaving all that they had ever known - was slowly eased. All around were pleased for them. Perhaps, some had thought, if Richard and Hannah could make a better life in America, then so might they too, one day.

   The children asked questions continually, seeking for reassurance as they could sense that these were times like no other. Each night before sunset, the family and others too would sit and listen. Richard would tell them about the native people that lived in America, called Indians. These primitive people had red skins, they wore eagle feathers in their hair, painted their faces, rode horses without saddles, and they belonged to tribes, such as the 'Sioux' and 'Apache.' Richard said that an Indian mother, named her child after the first thing that the child might see, such as a 'Crazy Horse,' or a 'Running Bear'. Richard added that they lived in homes made of animal skins, which were held up with long poles, and that they stood just like the 'stooks' of grain stalks did at home, at harvest time.

Richard explained to the children, "We cut down crops, and bundle together the stalks, and tie them around the middle. We then stand the stooks, with the heads of the stalks at the top, away from the ground. This stops the seeds from rotting before the stooks can be collected for threshing. Threshing is where we beat the stalks with sticks, which removes the seeds, ready for grinding for flour to make our bread". "It's hard work, and all the village helps out at Harvest time".

Richard continued with the tale about the Indians. Richard told that, "The Indians, who were savages, had fought with the early settlers, and they were mostly tamed now. At least in the east of America, which is where they were going to".

Richard told the children about their own mothers' relative, who had sailed to America already, some two hundred years earlier, aboard a little sailing ship, called the 'Mayflower'.

Hannah picked up the story, as it was her ancestor after all. Hannah told them that God had guided the 'pilgrims' to sail from Plymouth in England, and to sail to America, and Hannah added that God looked over the 'pilgrims,' once they had arrived on the east coast of America, at a place called Cape Cod. That place being so named, as the fish in the sea there, were called Cod, and they were so large and numerous, it was said that 'you could walk on their backs from ship to shore.' Hannah told them that God was looking over all of them too and was looking over grandfather John and their little sister Hannah, who had died in her second year, and also their brother Thomas, who'd died the same year as Grandfather John, with Thomas being in his thirteenth year. Richard listened to Hannah, and admired her for her faith, but Richard added nothing further.

Richard's father, John, had arranged for as many of the family as he could muster, from across Herefordshire, should come to a special gathering at the family church, in Staunton-on-Arrow. John had the Greenly family history written up, in the blank pages at the start of a large new bible, that he'd travelled to the city of Hereford to purchase. Richard was to take the bible with him to America, so that their story in England would never be lost. There were also blank pages for Richard to record the family history in America, the births, the deaths, the marriages, and the stories.

When all the family – from near and far – had gathered that warm and sunny day, John presented the bible to Richard. The Reverend of Staunton-on-Arrow, then blessed it, and he also blessed all that were gathered there too – both those who were leaving, and those who were staying.

Richard took a long breath and breathing slowly out, he smiled to himself. He gathered up his children close to himself and Hannah. Richard opened the bible, cleared his throat, and read. "The Greenly Family of Staunton-on-Arrow". "Descended from two noble Knight brothers, from the time of King Alfred. Then, from pre-medieval times, gentleman farmers of Staunton, Mowley and Titley, all small hamlets in the parish of Staunton-on-Arrow".

Richard swept his hand slowly around the church yard, indicating the many Greenlys buried there, and everyone looked around, and each thinking of their own dearest departed, and they each smiled respectfully. Richard continued. "Generations of our grandfathers and great grandfathers, all named John, and my own dear father John too, have worked this land for over five hundred years. With their bare hands, they cleared the woods, and they made the lanes we all walk along, by following in the footsteps of all the beasts who had gone before, and made a crooked path, all bent askew, over the years and years of their travels". The children looked down the lane, and understood now for the first time, why none of the lanes were straight. Richard finished. "They built our homes from the felled wood, and some of them, or their family, have travelled far and wide already".

Richard was the great storyteller in the family, and he loved nothing better than to pass on the family history through his learned stories as had happened many times over before. Richard learned the stories from his father and grandfather. Richard told the children of the ancient countryside parables, which were easy to remember and provide them a path. His favourites were 'from little acorns mighty oaks do grow' and being a blacksmith alongside his farming and woodworking skills, he would tell 'strike while the iron is hot' to teach the children to not delay when effort was needed.

The children interrupted Richard, "Tell us about the 'Great Fire of London' and our ancestor Phillip Greenly," pleaded the children. This was a favourite story of the children, but all the ages loved to hear Richard's telling of it. "Well now, let me see if I can remember it," said Richard slowly while smiling back at the excited children's faces. "A long, long, time ago in the year 1666, we weren't called 'Greenly' then, but we were called 'de Greneleye' instead", "Oh" said the children wonderingly, "And Phillip was called 'Phillipe' with an 'aeyy' sound at the end of his name", the children laughed, and the adults smiled, as if they were hearing this story for the first time. For all gathered knew it was to be the last time they would hear this story spoken from Richard's mouth. "Phillippe de Greneleye", continued Richard, emphasising each difference in the ancient pronunciation of the first and last names, "Had a successful slaughterhouse and butchers shop, right in the middle of the city of old London, in an area called 'The Shambles', and he also had a fine house, right near the great front doors of 'the old lady' herself, as all in London knew the great old wooden structure of Saint Paul's Cathedral". "Phillippe was called a 'Freeman of the City of London' and was held in high esteem by all that knew him, as was his wife, Alice". "Phillippe and Alice were both born here, in Staunton-on-Arrow, and buried just over there".

Richard pointed to a corner of the graveyard, and everyone looked and nodded solemnly. "He kept cattle on the fields just beyond the London City walls. The walls were first built by the Romans and surrounded the old city of Londinium, with the ends of the walls at the edge of the river, about a few miles apart. Each night, the seven great oak gates of the wall, were locked, and guarded over by the 'watch men', and no one could enter or leave".

Richard continued, "Late one night, in the first week of September, in the year 1666, a baker set fire to the bread that he was baking, and his whole shop was set ablaze. The bakery was in Pudding Lane. Of all the names, Pudding Lane", said Richard while gently shaking his head, and everyone laughed. Then Richard quickly changed his tone and pulled all of those listening back into the story, "The baker fled his shop, and the shop burned so fast, and so hot, that he couldn't put it out. The fire spread rapidly as the wind was strong and the wooden tiles and thatch on the roofs were tinder dry". Richard explained, adding drama to his telling of the story, "The houses stood so close that you could shake hands with your neighbour from the upstairs windows". Richard paused. "It was the middle of the night you see, and the only people working, were the bakers who were busy baking bread for the next morning's customers". "Fire, fire!", "Get out, get out, was screamed out all over", said Richard.

Richard then told that Philippe was also up early and had looked over the roof tops and saw a glow of red in the night sky". "Phillippe thought to himself that it was too early for sunrise which he had often seen and enjoyed from looking that way eastwards". Richard then told that Phillippe walked from his house, past the great doors of Saint Paul's, and onto his slaughterhouse in nearby Pincocke Lane. Phillippe, as he walked, was thinking about his dear brother Henry, who had died exactly one year before.

As Phillippe walked that night, he had noticed, in a bright moonlight, that the beasts were being walked in early, from the fields in the near distance, and just visible through a repair being made to the wall in places. The fields were owned by his farmer friend, in an area known as Spittal. Richard noted that the cattle were heading towards the Cripple Gate, as usual, for an early entry to the city the next morning. Once through the gate, in the morning, the cattle would be walked onwards the short distance to Phillippe's slaughterhouse, and soon after to his butcher shop nearby. Phillippe could get the best prices for the meat in the morning and was grateful that the heat of summer was over, and his meat would not be troubled by the flies.

Phillippe had also noticed that the cattle seemed somewhat agitated, which surprised him. He could hear the cattle moaning, whereas usually, they were walked in silently across the fields. Phillippe had also noticed that flecks of snow were falling from the sky and landing on his jacket sleeves, and that he couldn't brush them away, and added that he couldn't see too well, even though it was a full moonlight. There was something in the air, and Richard looked up at the obscured moon and smelled the burning just as the cattle had. "But that wasn't snow in September", said Richard. "It was ash from the fire", cried everyone who were listening. Everyone laughed at hearing, and so enjoying hearing, the story that final time.

When the laughter subsided, Richard hugged his father and mother, and thanked them for everything and especially for the bible which was written up with his and Hannah's, and the seven children's name, and also the two children who'd died. Richard read the entry aloud. Elizabeth, born in 1810, Richard born in 1811, Thomas born in 1815 and died in 1828, John born in 1816, Frances born in 1820, George born in 1824, James born in 1826, Hannah born in 1828 and died in 1830, and finally there was Thomas born in 1830. Richard looked at his children that would make the journey, and hand-in-hand with Hannah, and with their children they all walked the few steps across the church yard, to the graves of Thomas and Hannah, who'd both been taken so cruelly and so recently. Hannah cried as she held Thomas, still a babe-in-arms, and remembered her elder son Thomas who was buried where they now stood. They laid down the wildflowers that they'd picked earlier, and they laid some of the flowers on Grandfather John's grave too.

THE GREENLYS: HISTORICAL EYEWITNESSES 1415 - 1865

After a while, as they all walked away from that lovely old church, Richard's father John, thought to himself that Richard had not told the whole story of Phillippe and his wife Alice, as the whole family all walked past their gravestones too, which stood near the churchyard gate. And John also knew why it was that Richard hadn't told of the London inferno lasting four days and four nights. Nor did Richard tell of the inferno taking away his ancestor's slaughterhouse, or taking away his home and butchers shop too. And he hadn't told of his ancestor and his family and their servants numbly standing at the fires edge praying that it wouldn't take the old lady herself, and thinking to themselves, "Surely it wouldn't take the house of God".

Richard didn't tell that to his right-hand side, Phillippe could see down to the river Thames and the ancient London Bridge, with all of its wooden houses and all of its people looking over with great fear that the fire would come for them too. And he didn't tell that he stood next to a man who asked him if he'd lost. Nor that the man was none other than King Charles II, and with him was Samuel Pepys, who Phillipe knew well, as Samuel had offices nearby to conduct his affairs on behalf of the Navy. Samuel would drink and eat in the same local taverns as Phillippe. "That motley crew", Richard had said, speaking of Phillipe, Alice, their neighbours and the King and Samuel, "All watched as the 'Old Lady' at first smouldered, and hot ashes fell on those trying to save her books and relics". "Then the Old Lady's finger, which pointed up to God, erupted and burned and crackled so ferociously that it was like God himself was venting his fury". "Then it collapsed". "All had wept and wailed". "The King said quietly to no one in particular, 'God help us all'", and the King retreated into the dark night, such as it was. Samuel had stayed. He and Phillipe had stood most of the night, continually moving away as the heat and flames beat them ever further back and moved them closer towards the safety of the river. "What kind of God?", they both repeatedly asked of each other. But neither had dared to say what they felt.

John knew why Richard hadn't finished the story. And he also knew why none that were gathered had asked Richard to finish it either. And John also knew why, that of all his sons and his brothers' sons, totalling over fifty living close by, that it was Richard, and Richard alone, who was leaving.

PART THREE

THE ARRIVAL 1830

It was pleasantly warm in Philadelphia on the day of the Greenly family's arrival. Pennsylvania enjoyed a balanced climate of hot summers and moderate winters, ideal conditions for farming and not unlike Herefordshire in the better years. The Greenly family were welcomed ashore by a committee who then recorded their personal details and checked each of the family for any signs of disease. A deadly cholera had recently come ashore from one ship arrived from Northern Europe with German and Italian economic migrants and some French escaping the Revolution that started in France and was sweeping across Europe too. Anyone with even the slightest symptoms was taken away to a newly built hospital where they would be quarantined and hopefully recover, or more probably die.

Richard presented his testimonials and letters of introduction, that he'd kept safely on his person since leaving home. These important documents, which set out his character, were provided by the local reverend in Staunton-on-Arrow, and also by old William Greenly, the squire and the Lord of the Manor at Titley Court, which was just two miles down the lane from Staunton-on-Arrow. William Greenly, was a cousin who lived just a few miles away from Richard's own home, and William lived in an ancient and grand stately home. Richard and William both shared a common ancestor called 'John Greneleye' – the ancient spelling of the Greenly name

- from the Middle Ages, something that Richard's father John was proud to boast. "The first-born son is always called John since time immemorial" proclaimed Father John, with pride at himself being at the end of an exceedingly long ancestral line. Indeed, Richard's elder brother was called John being the first-born son. The 'Johns' of each generation were known thereabouts as 'the older' and 'the younger' to differentiate them.

Richard's brother John was prospering. Even in these challenging times. John, being the first born had inherited from his Grandfather John. Richard sometimes felt a resentment, but he kept that to himself. He couldn't change anything. Paternal inheritance to the first-born son was just how it was.

These English pioneer and settler families were welcomed as immigrants to America as they had been bought up under the guidance of The Church of England and were thought of therefore as having the highest morals and virtues, just as those on 'The Mayflower' generations before.

Richard couldn't have known that there had been recent trouble breaking out at all of the East coast ports. Trouble caused largely by the Irish immigrants who remained grouped around the same religious grounds that they had in Ireland; the Catholic and Protestants formed sectarian gangs and clashed violently. The locals were scared by the upheaval looming and rioted in all the big port cities, including New York and Philadelphia. They wanted the immigrants to go back to where they came from. Not just the Irish mind you, but the Germans and Italians and Chinese too. "They've brought all their troubles here and spew them out as either stinking disease or every other kind of trouble that we just don't want", said one of the committees heatedly. He continued, "They land and stay in their same groups and fight. And they live like pigs". "That's right", said another. "For supposedly God-fearing folk they behave like savages. Just like those heathen Indian tribes we've had to fight so long and hard to be clear of or at least tame as best we can".

Richard could sense Hannah and the children becoming unsettled on hearing these accounts. Richard himself felt unsettled too. They were already all exhausted and hungry from the weeks of sailing. They were frail too as they were mostly confined on the small ship and movement was limited.

This was a family used to being outside, and used to walking miles each day, as they tended their cattle and crops, or walked to the little village school that was opened by another cousin - William's daughter Elizabeth Greenly, or 'Eliza', as everyone knew her. Eliza married a Baron - Admiral Sir Isaac Coffin - who was himself an American, hailing from Boston, which was further north up the east coast from Philadelphia. Elizabeth had become Lady Elizabeth Greenly on that marriage. William and Elizabeth had insisted that Sir Isaac adopted the Greenly name and coat of arms. William had to seek special permission from the College of Heralds, and the King to do this. The 'college' maintained the records to show heraldic entitlement through a bloodline. College officers would travel around the country to see if existing claims needed to be updated, following a death for example.

Richard liked that Elizabeth retained the family name, as it was clear from the stories passed down through the ages, that his name was a noble name, and that Elizabeth wanted to preserve it.

Richard remembered that all the Greenly's from all around had gone to Saint Peter's Church, in Titley, to watch the wedding party arrive and leave. Richard looked at the stained glass in the church window and could see William Greenly's coat-of-arms there, which included stags with antlers. He could also see the family motto, 'Fal Y Gallo', which was Welsh, and meant 'As I Can'. William had inherited the arms and motto from his wife who had titles and estates in Wales nearby, which William inherited also.

John Greenly had been invited inside the Church to watch the ceremony. It was 1811 and Richard and Hannah had themselves married just two years earlier and shared the excitement of a wedding all over again. Albeit that theirs was a smaller one two miles back up the road at their family church in Staunton. Richard's father John had called Elizabeth "a bonny lass" and Richard agreed. Elizabeth looked calm and serene and clearly born to the manor. She looked very beautiful that day and Richard thought she looked like his own dear mother Jane.

His mother had always said half-jokingly, "I'm the beautiful wildflower meadow that your father needed to brighten his brown and dull landscape". My father would respond with his little story. "Now young lady. That brown landscape is where I toil hard with the plough and when I saw my seeds from my shoulder bag, I swing my arm in a broad cast and sing along, 'One for the rook, and one for the crow, and one to rot and one to grow'". Then looking at my mother he'd say with a questioning look, "Which one are you?" "The one for the Rook maybe", pausing slightly for effect, "or most likely the one to Rot. Yes, that's it 'the rotting one'".

My father and all would laugh so loud, and my mother would chase him off and he dodged about avoiding my mother's hands or broom or whatever else came to her hand. Eventually, panting and bent over with her hands on her knees my mother stopped her war cry, regained her breathing and joined in with the laughing.

Richard and his family were simple people who put their trust unquestionably in God and in the soil. They took nothing for granted. They knew that 'God works in mysterious ways his wonders to perform' and that the triumphs and disasters that lay on their path was ordained and each of those were to be treated just the same as they were 'Gods doing'.
Richard knew that if he were feeling weak then the children would be too. "Come on" he said brightly to the family. "Let's begin this wonderful time. Our new history will be written from this point forward. We have travelled and survived. And now we will thrive".

Richard and Hannah carefully gathered up their possessions from the dockside and were helped to find work and somewhere to live. It wasn't too long before Richard was working for a mining company in Pottsville a few miles from Philadelphia. His skills as a carpenter were in great demand and were used to good effect. He built and managed the sawmill that provided the timbers needed to shore up the mine's tunnels and the sleepers upon which to lay the new rail tracks that would transport the coal and timber back to the cities of the eastern seaboard.

Richard, and family, had arrived not too long after vast seams of coal, had been discovered in Pennsylvania. The story of the chance discovery of one particular kind of coal, was told to Richard as follows. Around the year 1800, a hunter was up in the wooded mountains, hunting for deer and bear, which were plentiful. The hunter traded in their skins. Each night the hunter would make a fire, which would be enclosed with the rocks and stones that lay around. This was to prevent the fire spreading by accident. The hunter cooked over the fire and slept alongside it, for warmth and also to keep any passing bears deterred.

The next morning, the hunter had noticed that some of the black rocks that he'd used, to contain the fire, were glowing red, and were hot to the touch, and stayed hot even after the fire was long dead. He filled a bag with these black rocks, and tried to sell them when he next went to a town, to sell his furs. But nobody was interested. The problem was that coal was already available, and plentiful and cheap. Massive seams of coal were already being mined all over Pennsylvania. And besides, and perhaps worse, these 'black rocks', that the hunter had with him, were hard to get alight.

Nonetheless though, once alight the 'rock coal', as some called it, would burn slowly, and with a more intense heat than the ordinary coal, which was already being used in homes and industry. Regardless of its advantages over 'common coal', no one had wanted it. Not yet at least.

Richard and his family were settling well into their new lives in Pottsville. Richard's skills and hard work were apparent, and he was promoted to the role of chief mining engineer. Richard's older sons joined him at the mine.

The younger children were soon settled at Pottsville's little school, and as children tend to do, they soon made friends with the other children. Hannah, meanwhile, also made friends with the other immigrant families, some of which were also recently arrived from England. Hannah also made friends with some American families, who'd also arrived as emigrants, but had now lived long enough in America to earn their right to American citizenship. The new friends would stand at the school's white painted picket fence and chat. The children would happily go to each other's homes after school.

Pottsville was far enough into the Pennsylvania countryside, that the locals would be spared the ugly scenes and hostilities, which were unfolding in the cities. Pottsville was one hundred miles inland, from both Pennsylvania and New York.

Richard regularly wrote letters home. He wrote with a confident copperplate italic hand, which he'd been commended on, during his school days. In one letter home Richard told that, 'no one much bothered to go to Pottsville, unless they wanted to go quickly underground to mine for the coal, or up into the mountains, to hunt for bears. Richard had told in his letters, how lovely this area was, enjoying vast tracts of trees, and wide and fast flowing rivers. Richard told them that he'd soon be looking to buy some land and forest, and start with farming again, just like his old life in Herefordshire. On reading these letters, Richard's father John, was comforted to know that the family were doing well, and that Richard was keen to keep his farming heritage alive.

Richard would later write again, stating that he'd 'met a gentlemen named James Leggett, who having arrived in America some years before the Greenly family, and had located in the vicinity of Millville, where he'd purchased a large tract of timberland. This area was known locally as Pine Township, in Columbia County'. James was having lumber manufactured in Millville, and he was hauling it by horse and wagon over the mountains fifty hard miles to Pottsville, at which place he found a good market for the lumber. It was used in the building of miner's cabins, and other small buildings, and the lumber was used by Richard too of course, as his own mill at the mine could not meet all the growing demands of those mines, and the growing town of Pottsville.

It was during one of these long trips to Pottsville, by Mr. Leggett, that he had met with Richard, and both had much to talk about pertaining to the past and the people in the land of their birth, and the outlook for the future, in this land of America.

Richard, being a man of ambition and of mechanical ability, told James that he was anxious to purchase and locate on a tract of timber where he could build a home, a waterpower sawmill, and become an independent lumberman and farmer himself. Having learned from Mr. Leggett that such a tract of timber could be purchased in Pine Township, Columbia County, Richard moved quickly to buy the land and move his family the fifty miles from Pottsville, to start their new lives in America proper. The year was 1835.

PART FOUR

LUMBERMAN, FARMER, AND WAR

Richard and his family built the sawmill that sat alongside the fast-flowing river. With that mill they built up a thriving lumber business, in Pine Township. They built a comfortable home, with plentiful timber too. The hardships of a few years before seemed far away, both emotionally, and in time and distance. The family received American citizenship and the children that had travelled found their own routine of life, which saw them marry and begin their own families. Most of Richard and Hannah's children and grandchildren stayed locally to that family-built home in Pine Township, and a few ventured a little further. These days were settled and good times for the family.

Richard retained his interest in the family history, and was to learn over the following years, while living in Pine Township, of other pioneers from the Greenly family who had also looked for new lives in America. And he also learned of the lives of his own father and mother, and brothers and sisters, and that of uncles and cousins, back in Herefordshire and wider places too. Richard would still gather the family, and now including some new American family and friends too, and would retell the old stories of England, and the new ones, with the details as he would learn them.

While Richard was of course interested in his own English history, he would also learn more about his adopted homes' history too; he'd learn of the early pilgrims – including Hannah's own ancestor – and he'd also learn of the history of England's rule in America, and he'd learn of the slaves that he saw all around, and how they'd come to be there, and why they were treated the way that they were. He would learn of the young nation of America, breaking violently away from their despised and distant English rulers. Richard would better understand why so many like others him and his family would make difficult journeys from England and many other places, and they too would travel with hope and great expectations.

Richard knew that his dear wife Hannah trusted in her faith, and she passed that faith onto her children too. Richard also had that faith, but he also had believed in himself, and his own ability to use his hands and heart, to literally 'make' a better life.

Whilst the early years of their settlement in Pine Township were busy, Richard still found the time, as he always had back in England, to gaze into a distant horizon and conjure up the stories. He would tell the stories in his own mind – so that he could recount them to all who would want to listen; he would see the stories with his mind–eye. He would see the people, he would see the locations, and he would hear the sounds and he would smell the smells, from wherever that story had taken him. And Richard would feel the feelings of the story's characters too.

Richard would think to himself, alongside these thoughts, that a man could live several lives in his own lifetime; a life connected to the past, a life of today, yesterday, and tomorrow where he'd need to eat and work and sustain himself and his family, and an everlasting life, when his time finally came, and he was called. Richard would wonder to himself why it was that the past mattered so much to him. And Richard thought about how wonderful it was that he could think the way that he did and share his stories. And he knew, from the expressions on the rows of faces who would gather to hear a story, that the past mattered to lots of others too. Richard thought to himself that the same happens in a church, and those that gather there to listen to stories of the past, and of their future depending on their conduct and behaviour. But even as he said it, he thought of his little daughter Hannah and of her brother Thomas, and he also thought about the 'old lady of London', and he thought of the young cousins Henry and Elizabeth. He thought of the crop failures and the recent hardship. Richard stopped and shook away those thoughts, as he knew that planting a seed in your mind needs careful nurturing, lest it grow rampant, and then could not be tamed.

Richard had been told in his younger years of two of the children of his great grandfather, John Greenly, who was born in Staunton-on-Arrow in 1683, and had lived the next eighty-five years there, until his death. That John had his place with all the other ancestors, in the churchyard of Saint Peter's Church, in Staunton-on-Arrow. This is the very same church where his family had all gathered to say their goodbyes to Richard and Hannah, years before. Great grandfather John had eight children, but Richard remembered the story of just two of them, Mary, and William. He already knew the story of the son of John, as he was his own father's grandfather, of whom Richard's father spoke often and fondly.

Richard sat and reflected on the story that he had heard from his grandfather, of Mary and William. Richard would have been around ten years old when he sat down with others to listen. Grandfather had said, "My dear father, John Greenly the elder, lived here the same as us today, and John and his wife had eight children. One of these children was Mary, whose own child left to live in America". Everyone listened, as to them, this was exciting to hear and far beyond their daily routine in Staunton-on-Arrow. The grandfather continued. "Mary Greenly married Stephen Watkins in 1738. Stephen was also from these parts, meaning Staunton-on-Arrow, and from a family of good and loyal friends for many years". "They had a son called John Watkins".

The grandfather interrupted himself to say all of these were resting in the village church yard and with their names and dates captured in the parish register. He continued, "Then there was Mary's brother William". Richard remembers interrupting, "Is that all about Mary?", he had said. "That's enough isn't it?", questioned grandfather. He explained, "It's to teach you about names and the wider family, so that you can all keep track of who's who, and who's gone where, you see". "Do you see?", he asked. Richard spoke up as he always did on behalf of the audience of listeners, "But why did Mary have to become a Watkins?" The grandfather sighed and stood up. "We'll continue this another day", and he then set off for home, and bit into an apple which he had had in his pocket. He turned around and called out with a mouthful of apple, "And remind me to tell you why we baptized you all with cider, in the church". He continued walking.

Little did Richard know at that time that he would meet a descendant of Mary, called John Watkins, in America many years later. Nor did he know that Richard and all around him living in America years later, would be swept up in a bloody and brutal war far away from this lovely place they all lived in now. That descendent of Mary was a soldier in that bloody and brutal war, and he had written home to his fiancée, with chilling eyewitness accounts of the story of 'The Battle of Knoxville', in the south of America in a state called Tennessee.

Richard watched his grandfather walking away for a while, and then chased after him. He held the hand of the old man, who he loved very dearly. "Grandfather", said Richard enquiringly, "What will my future be?". Without changing his walking pace, the grandfather just said, "Whatever and wherever, you will always be a 'Greenly'". And they both laughed. Grandfather broke a piece of the apple with his strong thumbs and gave it to Richard. Richard bit it and chewed it, and those two walked along saying nothing further, because they were both lost in their own thoughts.

PART FIVE

DISEASE AND DEATH

Disease and death could come at any time. And no one could escape. If it was your time, then it was your time. Or so it was said. Women often died in childbirth. Their children could be taken at any age. The feared ancient disease, and known as 'the plague', would come and go, taking many away with it, sometimes half of the people in a village. Richard could see from his travels around Herefordshire, that there were deserted villages, and crumbling churches. In these villages, which were abandoned in the 14th century after the plague had passed through and ravaged them, there was not enough people left alive to farm the fields and maintain the churches.

Phillippe Greneleye, the butcher, who had witnessed the Great Fire of London, had survived and lived through the last great plague in London which came in the year before the fire, that plague year being 1665. But Phillippe's poor brother, Henry Greenly, also a citizen and butcher of London, was taken by the plague in the month of September. September was the worst month of the whole plague. Henry's name was added to the parish register, which recorded the thousands who were taken in each parish in London. At first only a few names were added to each page, but as the months passed the names of the victims were written in a small text, so that they could fit all the names on the pages. 'Henry Greenly' was the very last name on the page for September and was written by a distressed hand in a tiny space in the bottom corner of that page. It was a pathetic last entry in all respects.

By 1666, the plague was finally leaving London, and many thought that it was the great fire that had finally finished it off. Some said, "god bless the great fire, lit by an Almighty flame". But the people were scared as they didn't know where 'the plague' had come from, or where it went or why it took some, but not others. It would take many months after the last death before people would begin to believe that the plague was finally done with them. Then a time for mourning, reflection and rebuilding would commence as confidence that better times lay ahead began to feel possible.

Each day of that plague year, Phillippe and his family would hear the terrible cry of "bring out your dead, bring out your dead". Phillippe watched the awful sight of the carts being pulled along the streets, with the victims piled there upon. Phillippe thought of his own wretched carts at his slaughterhouse, with the animals piled on them too. The families of the poor dead would follow along behind the cart if they were not too sick themselves. The cart would clatter along to the ditches and pits now being used to receive the bodies. The churchyards were already full, and because of the vast number of dead, and the urgency to have them buried, new burying pits were dug and even the existing city ditches were used. The family would do their best to see that their loved ones would find their way to God.

A church man, if one could be found, was willing, and able, would say a few words, but always from a safe distance, and then they would be quickly away. Many church men were dead already, as they were called to address the dying, and in the early days had gone to their parishioners but had succumbed to the disease. The church men no longer went to attend the dying in their homes.

The family would pay the cart man what they could afford and asked that he laid their loved ones to rest and plead that he did so with a gentle hand.

However, the families didn't stay to watch their beloved ones being laid to rest. For they knew that these days it would be a wretched scene. When the family had turned and were walking away, the cart man would tip the cart and then he pushed and prodded the tumbling bodies into the ditch. He worked with one hand on a rod, and one hand covering his mouth and nose with a cloth soaked in vinegar, to try and staunch the awful stench. Once the bodies were into the ditch, he then covered them lightly with a layer of soil. More bodies would be collected that day, and these would be added to the sorry heap.

There would be scavengers watching his work and waiting for him to finish and be away to collect more bodies. These scavengers were usually the old women who had no other means for support. They would climb down into the pile and take any clothes worth taking, but nobody wanted to buy these clothes anymore, no matter the price, as everyone knew where they'd been taken from. These burying ditches were at the edge of the old city walls, and to the east of it, to ensure that the prevailing winds would not bring the stench back westward to where the more prosperous lived in the villages, just on the outskirts of London, in places such as Fulham Bridge, Hamstead and Kensington. Henry Greenly was taken to the 'hounds ditch', which is where all the dead dogs of London and other dead animals were usually thrown, and where other dogs would scavenge in those piles.

Richard wondered about disease. He remembered, when he was aged about thirteen, in 1801, that Elizabeth Greenly, from that line of the Greenly family that had lived for hundreds of years at their family estate called 'Titley Court', had come, and scratched all the little children at the school in Titley, that she had herself founded. Elizabeth had scratched all the children to open a wound and draw blood, and Elizabeth had then wiped into the open wound, some of the white matter from the pustules that were visible on the hands of the village girls, who milked the cows from her families' own herds. Elizabeth was acting urgently, and many had wanted to stop her, but they deferred to her because of her and her father's position – who was now the Sheriff of Herefordshire - and because of her determination, for which she was known.

Richard knew that Elizabeth cared for the welfare and education of the local children, and that her motivation was positive. Elizabeth had provided a school and teachers, and even ensured that a meal was served each school day. Richard knew that she was trying to stop the children from getting an awful pox, but, just as everyone else at that time, he was not sure of the method being used. That 'awful' pox was called the smallpox, and that pox was just as deadly as the plague had been in earlier centuries. The plague had first arrived in the 13th century, via the ports on the south coast of England, and then it arrived again, every few generations after, including the latest and deadliest visitation in 1665.

People knew that the pox and plague were not the same disease; the plague caused black buboes on the neck and in the armpits to burst open, which is why some called the plague, 'The Black Death'. The pox caused the skin to burst out in smaller pustules all over a person, and some would be left with small pocks, or holes, on their faces.

Some years earlier, a man called Edward Jenner, who was a doctor in Gloucestershire, had noticed that the maids that did the milking of the cows, did not catch the deadly smallpox. He'd noticed they had white pustules on their hands. Jenner wondered if the 'cow pox', which caused only a mild sickness, was preventing the deadlier smallpox from taking hold. He wasn't sure how that could be though.

Jenner experimented with scratching some of the cow pox, which he thought must be present in the visible white pustules on the milk maid's hands, into the children's arms via a small wound that he'd opened. After a time had passed, and Edward could observe that the children had the symptoms of the mild cowpox, just as he'd expected, Jenner would then scratch in some smallpox, and to his delight he found that none of the children succumbed.

From this experiment, Jenner had asserted that a 'vaccination' – meaning in Latin 'from the cow' - of the weaker one, would prevent a person from catching the more serious other. There was a strong resistance to his assertion, with many arguing that it was against God's will to interfere. There was only a few who supported Jenner and who dared to conduct the vaccinations.

Elizabeth Greenly was one of those few who'd dared. Elizabeth, whilst a fervent religious believer, was also interested in science and industry, and befriended many of the leading thinkers, and emerging industrialists, of that age. This included befriending Jenner, who lived in a neighbouring county. Elizabeth received no formal advanced education, as was the practice in those days for daughters, unlike her father, who'd gone to Oxford University to study Law in 1760. However, Elizabeth was bright, and she pursued knowledge with a passion, and her father provided private tutors in Latin, French, Italian, music and painting in oils. Elizabeth became proficient in each of the subjects and had some of her oil paintings, of her beloved Herefordshire countryside, exhibited at the Royal Academy summer exhibition in London. John Constable and J.M.W Turner, who were two of the country's greatest living painters also exhibited at the same exhibition.

During the years of her life, Eliza collected many books that she kept in her oak lined library, at Titley Court. Some of the books were rare and valuable, with some manuscripts dating back to 1500.

Elizabeth's 'vaccination' of the local children was successful, and she recorded the success in the diary that she kept, for fifty years of her life, from age 14 years until just before her death. Richard had heard about the diary and knew that keeping a diary was quite rare at those times, and it was certainly not known for a woman to keep one. Elizabeth recorded her own experiences, and accounts of the fashion and politics of the day.

In 1860, Richard, who was now in his seventy-third year, had been in America for thirty years. Richard had built a good business and had put down good foundations in Pennsylvania, for the children, which came with him from England. But tension was growing in America. There were two major stress points. Some wanted the native Indians to be cleared from their lands and to be finally corralled into reservations, allowing for the businessmen from the East to build railways across to the West coast and open trading opportunities. And there was stress between those who wanted to retain ownership of slaves and those who wanted them to be freed.

America could be split into the northern states and the southern states. The southern states, had for generations, used Black slaves from Africa to work for the white owners' plantations of cotton or tobacco. These southern states feared for their future, as the President, Abraham Lincoln, was opposed to slavery and wanted it abolished, believing that 'all men are equal and should be free'.

The rift in views on the abolition of slaves, drawn along the north and south divide of states, would result in the American Civil War. The war started in 1861 and lasted for four long and hard years; the southern states effectively declaring themselves as a separate 'confederacy of states' and would no longer to be governed from Washington by President Abraham Lincoln.

Richard, and his wife Hannah, was still living in Pine Township, and was still farming there with two of his sons, James, and John. Over the next four years, Richard would see his sons drawn into the fighting on the side of the Union of northern states. Richard recalled that the American

THE GREENLYS: HISTORICAL EYEWITNESSES 1415 - 1865

President, called Abraham Lincoln, had visited Philadelphia in the second year of the war, where he and his family had arrived that warm spring day some 34 years earlier in 1830.

Richard had heard Lincoln address a vast crowd gathered, and Lincoln had said. "War, at its best, is terrible," "And this war is one of the most terrible". The President had said that they could not allow 'a few to remove themselves from the authority of the whole,' and that a 'United States' was to be the only outcome, regardless of the cost to all that were fighting for that end and fighting to achieve 'freedom for all men".

Richard's sons farmed with him and did not volunteer at the outset of the American Civil war. Rather, they focused on farming, and producing the crops that would be needed more than ever, to support the war effort and feed the Union Army of the north.

As Richard and his sons worked the fields in 1861 at the outset of the war, he told his sons about the days in Herefordshire, and the problems caused by the soldiers returning from fighting in the Napoleonic War. "England had been at war with France, on and off, for hundreds of years," said Richard. He continued, "Ever since the Battle of Hastings in 1066, and only finished when England defeated the little tyrant, Napoleon, at the Battle of Waterloo in 1815". Richard paused to let the two dates sink in. "It was the Duke of Wellington that beat his army," said Richard. He then added, "Just as Admiral Lord Horatio Nelson, had defeated his navy in 1805". "That was at the Battle of Trafalgar, off the southern coast of Spain". "It was a mighty sea battle". "The biggest sea battle since the Spanish Armada in 1588, when Sir Francis Drake saw the Spanish off", "But not until Sir Francis had finished his game of bowls". Richard and his sons laughed.

It was yet another sweltering day. The current heatwave had already lasted 40 days. Richard and his sons decided to take a break from the heat and their work, and to rest for a while under the shade of a tree, where they'd eat their lunch. Some cattle and some sheep were already under the tree too. The lunch, just as it was most days, was prepared by Richard's wife Hannah. Once a month, the three Greenlys would each lunch in a tavern in Hereford where they'd taken crops to be sold at the market.

Richard sat propped up against the trunk of the tree, and his sons sat on the ground opposite him. Their lunch was wrapped in a muslin cloth and included bread and butter, cheese, apples, pickles and with cider to wash it all down. Richard owned, as did many other around the area, a few apple trees that grew in his own orchard. The soil and climate were ideal for growing apples, and usually a single tree would provide dozens of excellent fruit. Each year, when the apples had ripened in the trees, they would load most of the apples in a cart, keeping a few behind, which would be stored and used for eating over the winter months. When loaded, the family would drive the cart of apples to Richard's father's large farmhouse, which was less than one mile from their own home, along a winding pathway. At his father's farmhouse they would use the pressing machine, to squeeze out the juice from the apples, which would ferment to produce the cider. Most families would drink cider rather than water, especially during hot spells of weather and when rainwater may not be collected. The pigs would eat the mulch left behind. Nothing was ever wasted on the farm.

As the three men ate and enjoyed their lunch, Richard told his sons proudly, "We were there". "Greenly's were at all of the battles". "Tell us again father," said the sons. Those sons still relished to hear the stories, just as they had done many times before.

"Where to start?" said Richard, as he always did when preparing the best starting place for each telling of the various stories. "Let me go back to the earliest battle, that I know of, and our deepest family roots in the north of England on the border with Scotland". "After the Romans had left England, there were other invaders called Vikings and Saxons, who wanted to rule England and make us their slaves". "Two of our Ancestors were brothers, and they were Knights". "Their names were 'Harold' and 'Athel' 'Greneleye'". Richard told them that the noble Knights lived in Northumberland and took their name from the place where they had lived for many years. "The brothers fought with King Alfred against the Danish Vikings". "As a reward they were given lands in Warwickshire".

Richard went on to tell his sons that those Greneleyes, and their families, had then moved south to those lands that were in the English Midlands, and where they prospered. Richard added that some of the ancient family had moved northwards and crossed the border to live in Scotland instead. Those Greenlys lived and owned lands around the south most walls of Edinburgh Castle. Richard added, having just realised the significance of the dates, "The Viking battle was in 850AD". "This year is 1860AD", he paused to let his bright sons draw out the conclusion. "So that is one thousand years have passed since then". Richard and his sons each thought about how long ago that was. They used the yard stick of the 30 years since they'd come to America, and which had seemed so long ago. The sons always said, 'come to America', whereas Richard always said it as, 'left behind home and family in Herefordshire'.

Richard drank some cider to freshen up his dry mouth. He carefully wiped his lips and told his sons, with immense pride, that an ancestor, 'Thomas Greneleye', had served as the Vice Chancellor of Oxford University in 1436 and then again in 1437. This fact had always intrigued Richard, ever since he was old enough to understand the meaning. He pondered often that an ancestor had been so significant, that he'd be equipped to be the head of such a noted seat of learning. "And" Richard went on, "We had ancestors at the battles that Henry V had fought with the French in 1415 too".

But the stories were not to be rushed, and Richard said they'd wait for another time when his son's own families could hear them too. He said to his sons. "Come on, we'll never plough the soil by turning it over in our minds". "Oh" he'd added, as they walked back to the fields, to continue their work, "I'll tell you too why we baptised you with cider back at home", meaning the home they'd left in Herefordshire.

Richard smiled, as he'd remembered his grandfather telling him 'The cider story'. Richard's mind wandered off, as it always did. He wondered if he'd have been brave enough to fight in a battle, or if he'd be clever enough to attend a university, to study and better himself. He thought that he'd been brave to leave home, and start anew, and that he was clever with his hands, and he could work with wood and soil. He also thought that he was clever in his mind, that he could recall and retell the history, both of the family, and, of the times and the circumstances that they lived in.

Because of the ever-present concern that France may try and invade England, Henry VII, had decreed in 1539, that all able-bodied men, aged over sixteen years old, from each village and town across England, were to be trained and armed ready to serve in Henry's army if and when a muster was called. The standing army had to be both 'willing and able.'

It was also decreed, that Beacons must be maintained on hilltops, and that these beacons be ready to be lit at all times. In the event that a mustering of the army was required, the beacon would be lit to summon the men from all the villages, and to make their way to the nearest market towns. It was around this time that Herefordshire men had been drafted to help with a rebellion, in the north of England.

The Greenly's own village of Staunton-on-Arrow, were to supply six 'billmen,' and one archer. Richard's ancestors were wealthy enough to provide a 'cote and salet'. A salet was the then name for a helmet, and a cote was the then name for a "coat of plates". This cote was the body armour that was usually worn by soldiers called 'billmen.' The billman must also maintain their own bill. A bill being a five yards long wooden stave, which stood as tall as two men. The bill was topped with a curved spike, sharpened along one edge, to the same cutting ability as a sword. It was the billmen who did the slaughtering on the battlefield, they were the executioners of the enemy.

Other families in Staunton-on-Arrow, were to hold 'at-the-ready,' two pairs of harness – to attach a cart to the horses, six more bills, three broad swords, four daggers, and a longbow, and plentiful arrows. The archer was Philip Greneleye. Philip was to practice his archery each week. He had to develop his strength to be able to draw the long bow and fire twelve arrows in one minute, and each arrow to travel over 400 yards. The other men of the village would all try and pull back the bow as far as Philip, but none could, such was the strength needed in the arms and the two fingers that drew the arrow back.

The Grenelye's had long been associated with providing soldiers and archers to fight for England, both the kind of archers that stood and fired their arrows into the far distance, to keep the enemy 'pinned down', and also the horse mounted archers who would fire their arrows a shorter distance, at the enemies own mounted archers. Greneleye archers had fought against the French at the Battle of Crecy, and again, under Henry V, at Harfleur and Agincourt, all battles taking place on French soil. The villages would also have to take with them hens, sheep, pigs, and cattle to provide food for the duration of the march and the war itself, and they would also take their own horses and carts.

PART SIX

KING HENRY V & WILLIAM SHAKESPEARE

Richard had cousins all around Staunton-on-Arrow, and he also had nine relatives that lived in the city of Hereford. These were the children, of the brothers of his father. His father visited them often, as the city of Hereford was just a few miles away, and could be reached in two hours on horseback, if the roads permitted travel. In those days roads were just compacted soil and would often be impossible to use following rain or snow. Richard had joined his father on the visits from an early age. Richard would ask his father lots of questions, to understand why it was that these 'Hereford' Greenlys did not work in the fields at home, like they did.

His father explained why this was so. "We farm the crops, and we raise the sheep, and the cattle". "We sell the crops, and we sell the wool". "And we sell the meat too". Richard agreed that they did. His father continued to explain. "Some of the families were skilled with their hands in ways other than farming or with wood, and they could make gloves from the animal skins we had". "They made the gloves while we worked in the fields". He then explained that those glove makers, eventually moved to the city of Hereford to set up as 'Glovers.' At that time, the city of Hereford, had a growing reputation as a place of excellence in the making of gloves. "A good living could be had". "Greenlys made the fine gloves worn by the highest ranks". "Other glovers made the tough working gloves, and the gauntlets for the soldiers".

Richard's father asked him, "Have you heard of King Henry V?" "Yes", said Richard, and added, "King Henry defeated the French". His father nodded to show his agreement and then added, "There is a play written about that King, and the war he made against the French, and it tells in part the story of our ancestors". "I'll tell you the story if you like". Even though Richard had heard this story time and time over, he still enjoyed it. In fact, he enjoyed it more with each telling, as he'd already made the pictures and sounds and smells relating to it in his mind. "Yes, please do tell". Richard replied.

John told the story of the play and their family. "The Greenly glovers, who lived and worked in Hereford, would sell their gloves from a glass fronted shop". "It was a smart shop, and fine customers would come to try the gloves, or some came to order ones especially". John explained. "Some may want gloves with their family crest or motto embroidered on. And some wanted dates of a special occasion". John went on. "But the Greenlys would also take their gloves to sell in the city of Worcester, where large markets were held on the feast days and the fair days". "Other glovers would travel there too, to ply their wares".

John continued and described an important meeting. "The Greenlys met and befriended another successful glover, and they both admired each other's work". "The other glover was named John Shakespeare, and he lived in a small town called Stratford-upon-Avon". "They each remarked that they both lived 'upon rivers', and that they'd each travelled twenty miles, with one travelling eastwards, and the other travelling westwards, to meet in the middle at the Worcester market".

John told more. "The traveller friends would talk about themselves and their families. It was as important to know a man's character two hundred years ago, just as it is today". John Shakespeare told of his family, and of a son, named William. William, liked to write poems and plays for entertainment". John Shakespeare added that William had ambitions to travel to London, and to act in plays there, until a time when his own plays were ready to be played at the theatres.

As part of the telling of their Greenly family history, the battles against the French, and the family's stories about those times was told, by the Greenly glovers.

"Our ancestors, are descended from two brother Knights, who had fought alongside King Alfred, in 850AD. A grateful King Alfred, awarded lands, called Balsal Heath, to the brothers". John Shakespeare interrupted to say that his ancestors had known of the family there, and that they were known by their ancient 'Greneleye' spelling. John added that some ancient royal records, were held at Aston Hall, which was built close to those Balsal Heath lands, and that those records showed the ownership of the lands". The Greenly glovers continued, "William Greneleye, had fought at the Battle of Crecy in 1346". "And that William's own ancestor had later served as a captain for Henry V, in the year 1415". "He was sixty-five years of age and formed part of the King's own personal bodyguard".

The Greenly glovers then continued to tell the story, with all its known facts added for completeness, as follows.

During the summer of 1415, King Henry V discussed, with his noblemen and advisors, the state of France and Henry's entitlement to rule over it. That same summer, a gift was delivered to Henry, from the French Dauphin, and delivered in person by his ambassador. The gift that the French Prince gave to King Henry was tennis balls. This was a cruel, and foolish jibe, aimed at Henry's youthfulness and specifically, at his regal inexperience. King Henry had flown into a rage. Henry ordered that the French ambassador be sent away. Henry and his nobles decided to prepare to wage a war, and satisfy Henry's claim to the French throne, a throne that he believed to be rightfully his, through his great grandfather, Edward III of England.

In September 1415, King Henry V, and his fleet of soldiers, embarked from Southampton, on the south coast of England. The fleet made its way across the English Channel and landed in northwest France. Once landed, the army followed Henry to the fortified town of Harfleur. Harfleur is situated at the head of the river Sienne, which runs from there into the city of Paris. Henry's forces lay siege to Harfleur. This fortress would provide a good place for Henry to rest his army, and prepare them to go further into France, and face the French Dauphin and his army, in a decisive, for both France and England, battle.

During the siege of Harfleur, Henry delivered a rousing speech to his soldiers: "Once more unto the breach, dear friends, once more!" The soldiers charged again on Harfleur's gates, and they take it as their own. Prior to Henry's speech, Sir William Greneleye, led his men to create a major breach of the gate in the high walls surrounding the town. It was this breach, that Henry V rallied his army to attack.

The Greenly glovers now told. "Here follows the full and true account, of the siege of Harfleur, and the breaching of the walls by Sir William de Greneleye".

They told that following the siege, the Greneleye family, based around Warwickshire, and living around the land granted some 500 years earlier, by King Alfred, were entitled by ordinance of Henry V, to have their Coat of Arms topped by a green mound and plant of Oak, such for glorious memorial to the Knight of the Royal Guards, "Guillaume Greneleye", who, while leading a storming and breach at Harfleur, and his seeing his Standard Bearer killed, and the Standard lost, plucked up a young oak plant, and called upon his troops to "follow a Greneleye and this plant to victory". Guillaume being an old spelling of William in the Middle Ages.

Whence William's soldiers cheered forward to the breach, which was gallantly captured, but within the fortress sorrowfully found their brave commander dying – with his last words begging his men to bury him on the Fortress Glacis (the mound of earth surrounding the walls), with the sprig of Oak, which had served for their Standard, to be planted over his grave; which command, the soldiers piously obeyed.

On the return of King Henry, at the close of the campaign, Henry, seeing the young oak flourishing over the green mound, where lay the valorous Greneleye, ordered the mound to be carefully turfed and fenced, and a slab built thereon, bearing the name Greneleye and the inscription "plus brave plus braver", which was the Greneleye motto, and also the Latin motto, "Fortes et fidelity". The King, also, as a further mark of gracious appreciation of his gallant Captain's service, on his return to London, ordered that the Royal Silversmith should furnish the Greneleye family, with a full service of silver plate, each piece with the family coat of arms.

There were two other Greneleye relatives of William, at Harfleur, they were mounted archers and went on to fight at the battle of Agincourt one month after the fall of Harfleur. Before the battle, those two Greneleyes, would once again hear King Henry rally his troops with another speech before the battle:
'We few; we happy few; we band of brothers! The man who sheds his blood with me shall be my brother; however humble he may be, this day will elevate his status'.

THE GREENLYS: HISTORICAL EYEWITNESSES 1415 - 1865

William Shakespeare's play, called Henry V, which described those days in 1415, was performed at Shakespeare's new theatre called 'The Globe' in 1600. This theatre was in Southwark, on the south side of the river Thames, in London. This play, in part, told of the achievement of William, in breaking the gates, and which Henry rallied his troops, with his call, "Once more unto the breach", in order that they may finish William's work, and take the town. Some Greenlys who were in London in 1600 went to see the play. These included the family that had travelled to London to attend the court of Sir Edward Coke inside Westminster Abbey. Sir Edward was to hear of a land dispute between brothers and he would rule on the case. Sir Edward's ruling was the 'common law' of England and would be referred to by other Judges who had similar cases before them.

John Shakespeare and those Greenly glove makers often discussed the play, and the growing fame and good fortune of John's son William, when they met over the years, and the parts that they had played in bringing it to the theatre.

PART SEVEN

THE AMERICAN CIVIL WAR (1861 – 1865)

Richard and Hannah sat at home with their sons one evening. It was late in the year 1863. They all sat quietly, and all were thoughtful. The American Civil War had already passed its second year. And just as President Lincoln had said, it was a 'terrible war'. Loss of lives and casualties for both armies was exceedingly high, and no one on either the Union or the Confederate sides had thought that the war would last so long. And whilst the armies had been made up of volunteers initially, the losses meant that fighting men would now have to be drafted in, and against the will of many of them and their families.

Richard's sons had received their draft notices and had set them upon the farmhouse kitchen table. Richard wondered why their lives were once again in turmoil. Over the past thirty years, since they had arrived, the family learned of other Greenlys that had come to America, most of them had come to Pennsylvania, but others had passed through and had settled in other states such as Ohio, Illinois, Kansas, and New Jersey and New York. Two brothers had gone south to the state of Arkansas. Ten Greenlys would fight for Pennsylvania. And Greenly would fight Greenly as the two southern most Greenlys had enlisted, or were conscripted, and would fight

THE GREENLYS: HISTORICAL EYEWITNESSES 1415 - 1865

for Arkansas, for the Confederate Army. Arkansas was their home and where they had a tobacco plantation.

Richard, wanting to build a full family history as always, researched the Greenlys involvement in the war. He found that over fifty Greenlys had fought for the Union and two for the Confederates. He also was to learn of John Watkins, the great-grandson of Mary Greenly, who provided an eyewitness account, recorded by his own hand.

It was a tearful and sad day as the family gathered to say goodbye to the new soldiers. There was none of the pomp and ceremonies enjoyed by the early volunteers. The bloody awful reality of war was soon apparent to those early soldiers. The newly conscripted armies, on both sides, knew that they were going to see 'hell itself', and soon.

John Watkins was the second great grandchild of Mary Greenly, who was the sister of Richard Greenly's great grandfather. There was bloodline there had thought Richard. John Watkins had served for the Union Army, and had signed up in Ohio, where his family lived. John enlisted in the 19th Ohio Light Artillery on August 9th 1862, as a Private. John was promoted to Corporal two months after. The Ohio unit participated in the 'Siege of Knoxville' and the 'Atlanta Campaign' before mustering out at Camp Cleveland, Ohio on June 27th 1865, when the war was over.

John Watkins was to meet up with the Greenly brothers, in Knoxville, Tennessee. The date was September 1863, and whilst John had seen active fighting for a year and more, the Greenly brothers went straight into it. They talked about their English roots and soon realised that they were both from the same family based around Staunton-on-Arrow in Herefordshire. They reflected on the coincidence, but as they grew to know each other better they could find similarities between them, in looks and manners.

John wrote letters home to his fiancée when he could. The Greenly brothers would have written home too, with the same shared story.

In one letter, John describes Knoxville to Sarah. "Knoxville must have been quite a place before the war began, but it looks now as though it was the oldest place in the world and been allowed to run down ever since it was built". He also mentions that Knoxville had contained a Confederate conscript camp, where the conscripts had to be confined "In order to hold them".

In another letter, John writes from Fort Sanders. This was a wooden fort which stood on a small hill, a few miles from Knoxville. "On the 20th of November, there was hardly any firing till dark. Then the rebels got another battery in position fired four- or five-times throwing shell clear over the town and bursting two hundred feet high. On the 21st it rained most all day and no fighting. The rebels had got clear round us from the river on the west side of the town to the river on the east side of town".

In the same letter John tells of a "sortie" made on November 24th by members of the 2nd Michigan to the Rebel rifle pits in front of the fort. After the 2nd Michigan was repulsed, a truce was called to retrieve the wounded, "Then you ought to have seen the rebel brutes rush out of the pits and strip the dead. Oh, if I ever felt like taking a man's hearts blood, it was them devils. And right in plain sight too".

John went on, in a further letter, to describe the awful battle.
In the frigid dawn of Sunday morning, November 29th, the expected Confederate assault came as four thousands of General Lafayette McLaws' veterans stormed up the hill.

John describes the attack on Fort Sanders. "Soon after daylight they opened on us from all their batteries or at least Five positions and if the shell didn't fly around us, I am no judge. The air was full of bursting shell but the most of them too high. I don't think that there was a man killed in the three quarters of an hour that they shelled us and, but one wounded and he was right beside us in a tent". "I was standing up against the breastwork and saw the shell coming just as plain as day. We could hear them coming before they got anywhere near us and what a noise they make."

"While this shelling was going on the rebels were forming for a charge on the fort and the first our folks knew of them, they were within twenty yards of the picket line and less than three hundred yards from the point of the fort". "And on they came with a yell, three columns deep and one in reserve", "the rebels came over logs, wire, and stumps and planted their colours right on the outer slope of the fort". "The slope there is on an angle of forty-five degrees and about twenty feet from the top of the work down to the top of the ditch. Then the ditch is about seven feet wide and six feet deep."

John describes the awful carnage, "They just piled in there on top of one another, dead, wounded and dying, and the living to get away from the fire of our troops. One of them got up to one of the embrasures with some four or five behind him in front of a piece that has three charges of canisters in it, and he hawed right out and says surrender you Yankee sons of bitches". "The words were hardly out of his mouth before the piece was pulled off and away went Mr. Reb and companions blown into ribbons."

"But all of this did not last more than half an hour for those that were alive in the ditches began to call for quarters and the order was given to cease firing". "There was an arrangement made right off to cease hostilities till seven o'clock in the evening."

"As soon as the firing stopped, I went up and got on the parapet to look at them. And such a sight I never saw before, nor do I care about seeing again. The ditch in places was almost full of them piled one on top of the other". "They were brave men. Most of them were Georgians. I would give one of the wounded a drink as quick as anybody if I had it. That is about the only thing they ask for when first wounded. But at the same time, I wished the whole Southern Confederacy was in that ditch in the same predicament."

The war finished in 1865 following the Confederacy surrender to the Union Army. Richard and Hannah welcomed their son's home and John returned to Ohio to marry Sarah. Richard thought back to Staunton-on-Arrow and the returning soldiers from the Napoleonic War. There was a difference this time he thought. Richard said to Hannah, "Back them it was Englishmen fighting the French in France. This time it was brother fighting against brother on their own lands".

PART EIGHT

JOHN GREENLY & THE BATTLE OF TRAFALGAR (1805)

Richard Greenly was born in 1787. A cousin, John Greenly, was born twelve miles away in the city of Hereford, nine years earlier in 1778. In 1796, when John was aged eighteen and Richard was nine, Richard and his father, and other members of the family, travelled to William Greenly's home to say farewell to his son, John, who was leaving to study at Christ Church College at Oxford University. The family all gathered in 'The Saracens Head Tavern', which was owned by William, and was where he ran his successful business as a corn and hop merchant.

On the journey into Hereford, John told Richard of another William Greenly who was a successful Vintner in London. "William Greenly was born in 1720 at Staunton-on-Arrow, and was the son of John, your great grandfather". "In 1741, at the age of twenty-one years old, William was apprenticed to Francis Fletcher, a citizen and Vintner of London - to learn his trade". "A Vintner being the importer and seller of wine", added John.

John explained that apprenticeships were usually for seven years, and usually commenced from the age of fourteen years. "They had considerable restrictions for the apprentice during that time. They couldn't drink or gamble and couldn't marry". "Effectively the apprentices were treated as servants – but they learned a good trade as their reward".

John finished the story. William successfully completed his apprenticeship in 1748 and was then able to trade as a Vintner for himself. On the 4th of February 1752, William married a girl from London, called Anne Beresford. The two were married at St Georges chapel in the fashionable parish of Mayfair & Westminster, in the west end of London. William was thirty-two and Anne was twenty-one years old. A relatively few Vintners would have controlled all of the import, and the sale of wine in London, and beyond.

William and his wife Anne were also the owners of the famous 'New Crown and Rolls Tavern', which was in Chancery Lane, in London. Chancery Lane was associated with the legal profession. The 'Society of Gentleman Practitioners', were the London lawmakers. Those 'gentlemen of law', met monthly at William's tavern. 'Mr Greenly, is to be trusted with the safe keeping of a trunk, which holds all the Societies papers and books', was recorded in the meeting notes of the first meeting.

William, being a Herefordshire man, also hosted the regular meeting of the Herefordshire Society, for the significant sons of Herefordshire that were in London at that time.

The tavern also hosted the popular 'card games', and these games were frequented by James Boswell and Samuel Johnson, who were two prominent characters of London. James Boswell, who was the 9th Laird of Auchinleck, he was a Scottish biographer, diarist, and lawyer, born in Edinburgh. He is best known for his biography of his dear friend, and older contemporary, the English writer Samuel Johnson. The biography was commonly said, at that time, to be the greatest biography written in the English language.

William Greenly died at the good age of seventy one years old, in 1791. William died at his tavern, and being a man of considerable standing, his death was widely covered in the London and Herefordshire newspapers. William was buried in the East Vault of the church called, 'St Dunstan in the West'. This church was a fine old medieval church. But it stood aside 'The Strand', which was an increasingly busy thoroughfare, for those travelling between the old city and growing west end of London. An Act of Parliament was obtained in July 1829, which authorised the demolition of the church, and trustees were appointed to carry it into effect. Auctions of some of the materials of the old church took place in December 1829 and September 1830. The first stone of the new church was laid in July 1831 and construction proceeded rapidly. In August 1832, the last part of the old church, which had been left as a screen between Fleet Street and the new work, was removed. The vault was left in place, and to this day, it still sits deep beneath the pavement of the newly widened Fleet Street. John concluded with a quip. "And so, a Greenly keeps close company with thousands of unsuspecting Londoners".

In the evening, they all attended a performance of musical works featuring Handel's Messiah. The venue was the Bishops Palace, which was a grand banqueting hall situated within the walls of Hereford Cathedral. This event was hosted by the Herefordshire Music Society. Edward Greenly, the glover and the father of Edward who had drowned, had organised the musical evening. Besides running his glove business, Edward was a writer in his spare time and held classes, at his home in the evenings, for those who wanted to learn the art from him.

The musical performance was also attended by Elizabeth Greenly, and her father William, from Titley Court. Elizabeth was keen to know which college John was to attend at Oxford, as her own father had studied there also. William told John that his days at Oxford would be the best days of his life. William also said that an Edward Greenly, had twice been the Vice Chancellor of Oxford University, in 1415 and then again in 1416. "And so, we Greenlys have big footsteps to follow", added William. John acknowledged the responsibility and thought he would not fail in his duties to gain his bachelor's degree.

William also added that through his own studies in law, that he'd read of the connection between the Staunton-on-Arrow Greenlys and his own Titley Court branch. William explained to John and Richard. "Our English Law is based on the work of a Sir Edward Coke who was born in 1552. He was a judge and asserted that a body of common law, based on the written-up cases already heard and decided upon by judges, should be the basis for all such future common cases and that the Royal's view that they should have the supreme decision was no longer defensible". "One of the many cases that Coke heard, and wrote up as his 'common law', was that of 'Greneleyes Case, which he heard and judges over in the year 1630'". William explained that this case involved some family members, two hundred years earlier, and that both sides of the family were mentioned in that case. William said that all of Coke's cases were written up in twenty volumes, and that these were at Oxford University, where he'd seen and read them.

THE GREENLYS: HISTORICAL EYEWITNESSES 1415 - 1865

Elizabeth, who was extremely interested in religion, was delighted to know that John intended to join the clergy after his graduation. Elizabeth would write a book of her own sermons, with one sermon for each day of the year.

Years later, the then 'Reverend John' would join Elizabeth, who was then 'Lady Elizabeth' and her Admiral husband, on a tour of HMS Victory which was docked at Portsmouth, on the south coast of England. HMS Victory being Lord Nelson's flagship, at the Battle of Trafalgar, and where Nelson destroyed the combined French and Spanish fleet of Napoleon. Cousin John, had served alongside Lord Admiral Horatio Nelson at that famous battle.

Richard remembers being mesmerised by the musical performance. The palace setting was grand and perfectly lit by many large candles, and Richard remembered almost gasping for air when the hallelujah chorus was sung. It was a night that he'd never forget. Later that evening, Richard with his father, and his Uncle William and cousin John, sat together in a room at William's tavern. There was a roaring log fire burning. Richard was close to the warmth of the fire and felt happily tired, being well fed, and watered too, but wanted to stay awake and listen as the elder ones talked. They discussed, as everyone always did, the threat of a French invasion.

William advised that following his studies at Oxford, John was to come back to Hereford and join the church as a Reverend. Much to his father's delight, John Greenly was appointed a Chaplain to the Royal Navy in 1804, and would serve under Lord Horatio Nelson, the Commander of the British Navy, who was himself, the son of a clergyman from a small village called Burnham Thorpe, on the north coast of Norfolk, which is a county in the east of England.

When Lord Nelson and John Greenly exchanged their family backgrounds on board HMS Victory, at a meal hosted by Nelson for all of the officers of his fleet, on an evening before the battle, Nelson had told him that his home was comfortable, and that he'd learned to sail, as a youngster, exploring the many creeks, that were around his home village. Nelson had said of Burnham, "It's not a place you pass through, so we didn't see many travellers".

Lord Nelson, thinking of his early school days, went on to say that he'd attended the old Norwich School, with his brother William. The school was set in the grounds of the fine and ancient Norwich Cathedral, and that the old chapel beside the Cathedral's great entrance doors was where the students ate, slept and learned. "That place filled my heart with a spirit to want to head out to the horizon and achieve the very best that I could for myself". Nelson continued, "I would stand and stare at the magnificent Cathedral and I would wonder in awe, at those men who'd conceived of it and had then built it, many hundreds of years previously". "I'd look to the very top of the mighty spire and thought of the man who had placed the very final stone and resolved that I too would reach the furthest that I could with my own life". Nelson added that the man had achieved something that he may not have thought of. That being that, as he stood atop the spire, that he'd been the closest man to God in the whole of Norfolk, and that he'd also the longest view of the county yet seen". Nelson laughed, and added, 'Norfolk is as flat as the sea".

The next morning, John and Richard made the short journey home to Staunton-on-Arrow to resume their farming lives. Richard was playing the music from the night before over and over in his head. He couldn't wait to share the evening with his mother and other family members. Richard was a great storyteller and mimic too. From an early age he'd mimic the sounds of the farm and of the nature he encountered around him. He would surprise his mother with the sound of a wild boar as she went about her daily chores. His mother would playfully scold him, and then she would embrace him dearly, for she loved that Richard had such a joy and zest for life. Richard could also recall the tunes that he'd heard. Consequently, all of those back at home would have an impression of the great musical works of the time.

As they made their journey home, Richard asked his father about the threat of an invasion coming from France. His father told him, without hesitation, that there was no need to worry, as there was no threat. He explained that our powerful Royal Navy, ruled the waves, as it had done for many years, and patrolled our coasts, to keep us safe. "That little tyrant would not dare", said Richard's father, defiantly. The little tyrant was, of course, Napoleon Bonaparte.

Neither Richard, nor his father, could have known that the very next year, in 1797, a small French force was to invade from the sea and land at the port of Fishguard, on the Welsh coast. Lady Elizabeth Greenly, had recorded the event in her diary. 'The invasion force of fifteen hundred was quickly confronted by the local population who took twelve hundred as prisoners, without any resistance. 'The French had said, after their capture, that they'd seen the locals dressed in their traditional Welsh jackets of red, and tall black hats, and had thought they were British troops, and had therefore surrendered'. The French force was supposed to invade at Bristol, on the English side of the river Severn, but could not get into the port because of bad weather. This, no doubt was much to the relief of the people of Bristol, as they had long feared, that if an invasion came, it would be via Bristol.

John later told Richard, "That failed French attempt was the only invasion of these lands, since William the Conqueror invaded the south coast of England, in 1066, and killed King Harold at the Battle of Hastings".

Richard was to next meet his cousin John in early 1805, when, once again, the family all met again in Hereford, at William's tavern, to see John set off on another adventure. This time, the recently ordained Reverend John Greenly, was to accept his position as a 'chaplain' on his first ship in Nelson's navy. The ship was called His Majesties Ship 'Revenge'. The mood of the gathering this time was serious, as all knew that a major sea battle with the French and Spanish was looming, and that John would be a part of that. "History will be made", had said John's father.

When the Greenly family had next gathered again, it was early in the Spring season of 1806. They had gathered to hear the eyewitness account from the Reverend John, who was twenty-seven years old by that time. All the family and many more wanted to hear of the 'glorious victory' achieved, against the combined Spanish and French fleet. The victory, which was won a few months earlier, was still being celebrated joyously, in all corners of England. The looming threat of a French invasion, which had so worried the nation for years, was at last ended. Napoleon would finally be defeated, on his home soil, years later.

Those who had served at The Battle of Trafalgar, and particularly those who had served and had written up the account, were regarded as national heroes, and received a grateful adoration, wherever they went. Reverend John, like Richard, was an accomplished storyteller too, which further elevated his standing among those who had served.

Reverend John shared the handsome features of the Greenly men, and Richard had thought that of all the family, it was Reverend John who most resembled the ancient portraits of the Greenly cousins, that he'd seen, on a visit to Titley Court. Richard had gone there to speak with Eliza Greenly, regarding a new breed of cattle that she wanted to add to the 'Hereford' breed that were common around the fields. Richard remembered that there were five portraits there, and that they were displayed together in large gold frames, and hung against a deep scarlet papered wall, which was just near the doorway to the great library. Eliza had stopped by them as she anticipated Richard's interest. Richard asked Eliza who they were. Eliza went through each portrait and indicated that each frame included a little plaque that showed the names and their dates of birth and death.

The first portrait that Eliza described was Dorothy Greenly (1610 - 1702), who was the daughter of Edward and Elizabeth Greenly of Titley Court. This showed a portrait of a rather stern looking face, but the Greenly features were clear to see. The second portrait that Eliza described, was John Greenly (1641 – 1729). This was a fine-looking man with a full powdered wig and wearing a gold jacket with a royal blue silk lining. Richard said to Eliza that the look of the eyes was extraordinarily strong. Thirdly, Eliza showed a portrait of herself, and, next to hers, she showed the portrait of her father, William.

Eliza also showed a miniature portrait of herself that had been commissioned by her dear mother. Richard held the miniature portrait carefully, almost tenderly. Richard rested it on the palm of his hand and brought his hand up to his eyes and observed it closely. Although it was only two inches tall, it captured Eliza perfectly and Richard saw a lovely and serene face looking back at him. He could hardly conceive how this had been achieved, with paint and brush being mastered onto such a small space. Eliza explained that a single bristle was used to create the detail. Lastly, there was an exceptionally fine portrait of Anne Greenly and which had been painted by the famous artist, Thomas Gainsborough. This face was just as serene and beautiful as Eliza was.

When everyone that had gathered, had finished enjoying the splendid food and drink that had been provided by William, John slowly pushed his chair back along the wooden floorboards. Then he stood up from his chair, which was at the head of a large oak table, and all gathered eagerly anticipated the telling of his eye-witness account. John started, "Before I begin to tell of the glorious victory, please all join me in toasting our beloved commander who led us bravely to victory and who paid the highest price in that bloody battle". All that were gathered, who numbered fifty, stood, and raised their drinks and joined John as he raised his own glass and toasted, "Lord Admiral Horatio Nelson, our deeply lamented, beloved and adored hero". All repeated the toast.

There then followed a call from all at the table for 'three cheers', and a rousing 'hip hip hooray' rang out around the room and into the streets of Hereford. News of the gathering, for their local hero John, had quickly spread around the city, and many were in the street outside, to share in the celebrations. Inside the room, the cheers from the street could also be heard. The mood all around, both inside and outside, was highly charged and excited.

John stood quietly and all around settled into a silence too. John who had a 'rich voice and a rare ability to command a good sermon', began his account. "Just two years ago I proudly joined His Majesties Royal Navy as a Chaplain, to tend to the spiritual needs of my shipmates; both the Officers and also the 'Jack Tars' below deck. John explained that a 'tar' was a nickname for the common sailor who would all be involved in applying the black pitch to waterproof the boards of the hull. "I joined my first ship in early 1805. It was called HMS 'Revenge'. She was newly built and anchored in the river Medway, just offshore from the naval boatyards at Chatham in Kent. It was a fine seventy-four gunner and was very manoeuvrable". John explained the layout of the ship and its crew. "A crew of eight tars each managed a gun. They would all sleep next to the gun in their mess and were always ready for battle". John continued, "These eight tars were 'mess mates', and would take a turn to prepare the meals of oats and ale".

He then went to explain that all on board and across the whole fleet, knew that the very future of England depended on the outcome of the battle. The English foreign agents had reported that there were hundreds of small flat-bottomed boats along the French coast, and that these were ready to transport a French invasion led by 'the little tyrant' Napoleon. But Napoleon needed the seas to be cleared of the British Navy first.

John prepared the gathering for the story. He began by giving a sketch summary of the scene, from which he would colour in the details to paint the most vivid picture that he could. Richard was as interested in how the story was being told as the actual story itself.

John began. "Late last year, on Monday 21st October 1805, off Cape Trafalgar, Admiral Lord Nelson, with 27 ships of the line, attacked the 33 ships of the combined French and Spanish fleets under the command of Vice Admiral Villeneuve. Firing started at midday and by tea-time the most famous sea battle in British history was over. Napoleon's fleet had been virtually annihilated with 17 ships captured". "50,000 men took part; around 15,000 were killed or wounded, mostly on the French side". "Britain lost not one ship. But she had lost her hero, and most celebrated naval commander."

John then held up two letters and explained them. "These two letters were written by my own hand, to my father William, and they bear my witness to this illustrious historical chapter in England's long history". "I shall read out each of these letters for you". John paused and then continued. "The first letter was written on the evening immediately following the battle". William, who was seated proudly next to John, added, "Do you see? It has some blood that was shed by my dear John".

John settled his father down, who'd become quite stirred, and then read out the letter. All of those who listened to John could also see each word relived in the face of their own hero.

"Off Trafalgar. October 21st, 1805. 'A glorious day for England'." "Dear Father, I have this day witnessed a scene, which I suppose you have seen described in the papers, yet I shall not lose the opportunity of a cutter's going to England from Lord Nelson; such news has not been heard since the Spanish Armada. We discovered the Enemy (which I am glad I first saw) at four o'clock in the morning. Forty-one large ships. We had twenty-six sail of the line with light breezes. Lord Nelson made the signal to engage the centre of the enemy, which Admiral Collingwood did in a most gallant manner and cut off twelve of the enemy, which three of ours engaged, the 'Revenge' led them, & I am glad to say has immortalised our good Captain".

"I will tell you the result of this glorious action. We have sixteen in tow, and one four-decker - rather an unusual ship, one is blown up, & one is sunk by the 'Victory', Lord Nelsons' ship, which you may be sure, behaved as he always does".

"The last signal Nelson made by telegraph was, "England expects everything from this day's action, and trusts every man will do his duty".

"Our Captain told his men, we would act as Lord Nelson had always done, lay his ship alongside the largest he came near & would leave the rest to his men. They gave him three cheers, & they fought like lions. The 'Revenge', a fine seventy-four, had four seventy-fours & a three-decker at one time upon her".

"We are terribly mauled, we are almost a wreck, but we made two seventy-fours strike & drove off the three-decker, then Lord Nelson who was close to us, cheered & we cheered in return & immediately the 'Victory' sent one to the bottom & every soul perished".

"The ships on both sides fought very hard but the coolness of Englishmen showed them what they had to trust to. The enemy had eleven sail of the line more than we had, three frigates & a brig. Admiral Louis with seven sail of the line left us about a week ago to water at Tetuan; but the fewer in number the more honour & profit".

"I had a very narrow escape, a forty-two pounder came within six inches of me & entirely shattered a beam: the Captain ordered me off twice, but I went up when I could from the wounded. We had a dreadful carnage: Captain Moorsom (very slightly wounded in the cheek but would not quit the deck) fought as coolly as if at dinner, never less than two on us from one o'clock midday till half past six. We have twenty-seven killed & forty-five wounded very badly, some of the "Centurion's" late crew, our Master is wounded, two Midshipmen killed, two wounded, all our yards were shot away & topmasts & lower masts terribly mauled. The killed onboard the enemy must have been dreadful, as one of the ships which struck to us was employed all the morning in throwing their dead bodies overboard. We were so disabled that we could not take possession of our Prizes, the "Polyphemus" & another have got them astern of them".

"I would not have been out of this action for any consideration, though the sight of the dead & dying are dreadful. We do not know where we are going to, but somewhere we must go to repair our damages & with our Prizes. We are in high spirits & trust you will all think well of British Tars, many of whom died in my arms cheering their messmates above. Lord Nelson is wounded; he is obliged to leave the deck". "Believe me, Yours truly, J. Greenly".

John explained the key points in some detail. He used some of the crockery and cutlery on the table to show how the two fleets were positioned, and how his brave 'Revenge', had been one of the first to break the line of the enemy. He talked about his work below deck, where he supported the surgeon, and gave the last rites to some of the twenty eight who were killed, and he gave comfort to some of the fifty five who were seriously injured. John and all those gathered, stood, and raised a glass to his fallen shipmates.

John explained that good commander Nelson had survived until he was told of the victory. John explained that he'd written his last words in a second letter to his father, which was written a week after the battle. John held up the second letter.

THE GREENLYS: HISTORICAL EYEWITNESSES 1415 - 1865

"Off Cape St. Mary's, Oct 28th, 1805."

"Dear Father, in my last to you, I told you a few of the Ships taken, but I have now to tell you of 21 sail of the line, most of them burnt & destroyed, as we have had complete gale of wind since the action. I hope all our ships are safe, many of them are totally dismantled - we ourselves are in a terrible state, but owing to the exertions of the Ship's Company, we are in a state to keep to sea. Two Spanish three deckers burnt, & four Admirals taken. We have bought the Victory dearly, as our brave Commander died of his wounds the night of the action - his dying words were, "I die happy, never was there so grand a day for England, nor Englishmen behaved better". There has been dreadful slaughter on board the "Revenge" and "Victory", "Bellisle", "Tonnant" & "Royal Sovereign."

"I was wounded in twenty places by splinters of shot that came close to me, but mere scratches; its rather an unusual thing for a Chaplain to be wounded in action, but mine were so slight that I would not be put in the list of wounded. Our ship is full of French & Spanish which we took out of the Prizes - Captain Moorsom was complimented by Admiral Nelson on the evening of the action & sent to enquire if he was well & to lead the English down again to destroy the enemy".

"If the wind had not come on to a furious gale, we had not left a French or Spanish ship in existence: as it is we have but destroyed twenty-one sail for certain - all very large ships: the gale still continues but is all clear of danger: the loss of prize money will be great, as had the wind permitted us to have brought the ships home I should have had £500 - but now not £20, though we are glad to have lowered their pride. We are all in good spirits, though no sleep for three nights".

"Poor Lord Nelsons' body will be brought home - the people of England have got as fine a man, old Cuddy Collingwood who led us down like a Lion & is close to our ship now. I have no time for more. Yours affectionately, J. Greenly. N.B. The Spanish & French must have lost more than six thousand men".

John explained that the enemy's loss was closer to fifteen thousands, once all the reckoning had been done. Finally, John told of Lieutenant Lewis Hole, who was a friend who had served alongside him, and that while John would write his accounts Lewis would paint the scenes as small water colours.

John passed around a small watercolour showing the Revenge surrounded by three French and one Spanish ship, with all guns smoking.

THE GREENLYS: HISTORICAL EYEWITNESSES 1415 - 1865

The painting was carefully passed from person to person around the table, who all regarded it thoughtfully, and eventually it was passed back to John. John folded the letters and the watercolour and placed them carefully in a leather pouch. He buckled the pouch and placed it on the table. He stood quietly for a few moments as if the buckling was an end of the story, at least for this occasion.

At this point John sat down. All that were gathered then cheered for him. When all the congratulations had settled, John went on to inform that he had attended the funeral of Nelson and gave a description.
"Our commander's body was brought back to England on board HMS Victory, and he was buried at St Paul's Cathedral."

"Lord Nelson's funeral was the grandest state occasion the nation had ever seen and lasted over five days. As he had requested, his body was placed in a coffin made from the mast of the French ship, L'Orient, destroyed during his famous victory at the Battle of the Nile. Nelson's undress coat, which he had been wearing when he was shot, was returned to his dear Emma Hamilton, in accordance with his wishes".

"Arriving at Greenwich, on the river Thames, on 23 December 1805, his body lay in state in the Painted Hall from the 5th to 7th January 1806. More than fifteen thousand people came to pay their respects and many more were turned away. Nelson's body was then taken from Greenwich up the river Thames to Whitehall on 8th January, spending the night there before the funeral at the Admiralty. The next day it was placed in a funeral car, modelled on the 'Victory', and taken through the streets to St Paul's Cathedral. Sir Peter Parker, Admiral of the Fleet, led the mourners, and members of the Victory's crew were in the procession".

"The service at Saint Pauls was charged with emotion, marking the passing of the man who had delivered his country from a foreign threat. Thousands watched as Nelson's coffin was lowered down and laid to rest in an ornate tomb in the crypt of Saint Paul's. The tomb is now surrounded by the graves of many other naval officers".

Richard was drawn to thoughts about the other Greenly story, about the Great Fire of London, which had burned down the old Saint Pauls church in 1666.

William's father spoke. "Let us all go into the street and meet the well-wishers". The gathering all went outside and hoisted John up and onto their shoulders. Richard remembers that the whole of Saint Martin Street was full of cheering crowds, who had decorated themselves with flags, and even the ancient bridge over the river Wye was crowded too. John was carried to the centre of the bridge. All were cheering. All were trying to touch his hand or clothing. John looked over the bridge and down to the river and could see that it was full of barges. And all on those barges were standing and were cheering and waving flags too.

John held a mouth-trumpet to address the crowd. These 'trumpets' were used on a ship to raise a voice above the sound of the wind and were also used at the height of a battle. But John remembered that the battle had been so loud, with the cannons firing and wood shattering all around, that all on board were effectively stone death for the duration of the battle, and in some cases, for many hours afterwards. John held the trumpet to his mouth and shouting into it he shared Nelson's last signal. "England expects everything from this day's action and trusts every man will do his duty". All cheered wildly.

John then shared Nelson's last words. "I die happy, never was there so grand a day for England, nor Englishmen behaved better". All that had gathered felt their emotions swell up, with a mixture of sorrow, pride, and eternal gratitude that Nelson had defeated Napoleon's fleets. And here before them, was one of their own, a man from the city of Hereford, and one of the few who'd been there and seen it all and had lived to tell the tale.

As they walked back to the tavern, the crowd threw their flowers and William proudly looked at his son but could see that he had received injuries more serious than he'd said in his letters. Later, John would receive a handsome lifetime pension, paid for by a grateful nation.

In later years, John wrote a diary and included an account of the battle and would tell of the men who'd served and fought alongside him, and how it was that many were 'taken' against their will, and were forced to join the Navy, but nonetheless, those brave Tars had fought like lions, despite the dreadful conditions and treatment that they received.

He would also tell of the story poor Jeanette, a new bride who smuggled herself abroad a French ship. Jeanette's new husband, who was her childhood sweetheart called Etienne, had been taken from a port on the south coast of France, on the day of their wedding. Jeannette was plucked from the sea by the English sailors as her French ship was sunk and she only just managed to escape. Jeanette could not swim and was survived by clinging to driftwood. The water was cold as it was late October. John met Jeannette as she was taken onboard the Revenge. John gave up his quarters so that Jeanette could be private. Jeanette eventually made her way back home from England after the Revenge had docked back at England.

Just as in England, the Navy's of Europe would all 'press' any boys and men that they could find, in and around the ports, and sometimes from nearby villages in shore. The 'taken' were thrown into the ships hold, and one of their hands was tied to a beam. These souls would remain as captives until the ship was out at sea. The taken had no choice but to accept their fate. Punishment was brutal and so all kept themselves quiet. A Tar could only speak to an officer with, 'Aye Aye, Sir.' However, they spoke more freely with the Reverend John. But these stories were for a later time, as all now wanted to focus on the victory and the heroes, and not on how much the victory had cost to the many who had served.

Reverend John married Mary Prosser, who was also from Herefordshire. They married in the city of Hereford in 1809. They moved from Hereford to live out their lives, over the next fifty years, in the rarefied sanctuary of 'The Close', which was a collection of fine houses built specifically for the clergy and situated within the walls of the magnificent Salisbury Cathedral in Wiltshire, in the south of England. John performed clergy duties as the Vicar of The Close. He also ran the Grammar School from his large house. The school could accommodate forty paying students as boarders, and the students were also the choristers for the Cathedral.
In 1811, Reverend John met a visiting celebrity to the Cathedral who was called John Constable. The famous landscape painter had come to Salisbury, to sketch views of the mighty gothic Cathedral, that he would later paint in oils.

PART NINE

SALISBURY CATHEDRAL AND JOHN CONSTABLE

The two Johns were of a similar age and became friends, with John Constable staying at John's comfortable home in the Cathedral Close when he visited.

Both were great admirers of each other; one for the others magnificent paintings, and the other for one who'd been present at a defining moment in English history and could describe it so vividly. They both wondered whose work would live the longest in the nations interest.

John Constable visited Salisbury a number of times over the following years. He'd spend his days sketching more views of the Cathedral, from different viewpoints and with different skies, and he would produce small watercolours. These would become his studies for his final paintings. There were two major works of the Cathedral, and these were exhibited at the Royal Academy exhibition, and viewed and admired, by many of the great in society. The two paintings were a view of the Cathedral from the meadows, and a view of the Cathedral from the Bishops Grounds. In the latter painting there are two small figures in the foreground, a male and a female. John told his friend that these two figures were John, and his dear wife Mary.

In the evenings, the two Johns would share a drink and talk about Nelson and Trafalgar. John Constable said that another painter, named Turner, who had previously painted magnificent scenes depicting the battle, was now painting a solemn picture of HMS 'Temeraire', being towed away for scrapping. That ship had been at Trafalgar too. John added that it seemed a strange choice for such a heroic vessel.

John Greenly lived in The Close at the Cathedral, for fifty years, until his death in 1862 at the age of eighty-five years old. His life there is commemorated on a plaque close to his burial place; it tells of a tragedy that swept through his family in 1855 when four of his young grandchildren died in John's home within the space of a month. Cholera was rife in Salisbury at that time.

PART TEN

LADY ELIZABETH GREENLY

REGENCY DIARIST (1771 – 1839)

Elizabeth Greenly was born in 1771 at her family's ancestral home, Titley Court in Herefordshire, to Elizabeth May Brown, age nineteen, and William Greenly, age thirty-one years old.

    Elizabeth, or Eliza as she preferred to be called by those that knew her well, was a distant cousin of Richard Greenly. Eliza was 15 years old when Richard was born. Eliza and Richard were related via a common ancestor, John Greneleye, from the early 16th Century. During the following three hundred years the two family branches lived within two miles of each other. Elizabeth and her ancestors lived in Titley Court, the large Manor House in the village of Titley, and Richard's ancestors lived in and around the nearby villages of Staunton-on-Arrow, Kingsland and later Eardisland.

    Eliza, as was so well captured in her portraits, was an attractive and serene looking woman. All whom she knew, which included anyone regardless of status, found her charming, interested, and inquisitive. Throughout her life she met and associated with many characters of the Regency period, including the Prince Regent and other members of the Royal family. As we'll see from reading her diary entries below, she looked young for her years. We'll also see that she had a great love for children although sadly she married late and had none of her own. Eliza had an extraordinarily rich life, both materially and intellectually. She met many interesting people and also experienced many interesting events. Her friends would also recall their own experiences for her too. Unfortunately, as we'll read, Eliza's marriage was largely an unhappy time in her life.

Eliza kept a diary from the age of fourteen years old. This was a detailed year by year account of the comings, goings, and doings of Eliza from the year 1784 to within six months of her death in the year 1839, at which time Richard had been in America for nine years.

Richard and Eliza lived just two miles apart from each other, and Richard would often talk with Eliza about her diary and the experiences that she'd recorded in it. In fact, being sixteen years her junior, Richard's children had attended the school that she founded, in her home village of Titley. Eliza had thought that Richard had the same passion for enquiry and learning just as she had too.

Eliza also recorded in her diary, the details from family letters from before her birth, and from her childhood, that were in her possession following the death of her maternal Grandmother. There follows an account of some of the Floyer family.

Mrs. Hughes was my Uncle Floyer's sister. She survived my Aunt Floyer by some years, and used to be much with us when we were at our house in Abergavenny, always dining with us on Sundays. She was a fine upright figure, six feet without her shoes, and must have been very handsome in her youth. She was delicately fair, was a pattern of neatness and preserved all of her faculties to the last. She lived to be ninety years old, and she often related to me anecdotes of former times. Among others, she told me she remembered seeing an Aunt of her husband's (who had been a great beauty and who had danced at Court in the reign of Charles II), who, at the age of one hundred and three years old, was stitching the wristbands of a fine holland shirt without spectacles – she lived to be one hundred and fifteen years of age.

Mrs. Hughes's and my Uncle Floyer's grandfather, John Floyer, Esquire, of Whitehouse, was left at twelve years old to the guardianship of his relative, Mr. Hughes of Trostrey, who one day asked him which of his daughters he would have for a wife. "Would he have the eldest", "No". He would have his cousin Mary, a girl of eleven years old. The father took him at his word, and considering it an advantageous match for his daughter, actually had the marriage ceremony performed, and then sent the boy and girl to school. At holidays they met, but no one looked upon them in any light but as children, till an evening when the whole party were at high romps, the juvenile wife was seized with the colic. Her playfellows rolled her on the hall table, a popular remedy in those days for the disorder, but as it was not removed, more experienced Doctresses were called in, and in a brief time, a fine boy, Mr. Floyer's father, came into the world.

June 24th 1783. Eliza, when aged eleven years old, visited Windsor with her parents. We went to Windsor to pass a few days with the Dean and Mrs. Harley. With them we drove one morning to Ascot Heath Races, attended by the Royal Chapel each day, and every evening we walked on the Terrace where we were sure to see the Royal family. One evening, the King stopped and spoke to the Dean and described to him an accident that had happened to Colonel Fane, Lord Westmorland's brother, who walking backwards and engaged in conversation with some ladies, came unawares against the low parapet wall at the end of the Terrace, lost his balance and fell back over the wall; but was providentially caught in some bushes. The King looked towards us and asked, "Who's that?". "Mr. Greenly and family", replied the Dean. "What, the Greenlys of Kingston?" "No, please your Majesty", said the Dean, "The Greenly's of Herefordshire". "Oh", said the King, and then added, "I know them".

On the way home we stayed a couple of days at Oxford, at The Star Tavern, and dined on one of the days with Mr. John Foley. The meal was hosted at Brazen Nose College, which is one of the oldest colleges at Oxford. Mr. Foley is an old friend of my father's, who took pains to show us most of the objects most worthy our regard in the University. 'Brazen Nose' got its unusual name from a twelfth century 'brazen', meaning brass, door knocker in the shape of a nose.

Eliza shared a first-hand account of the 'balloon fever' that was gripping London. The letter was from Eliza's cousin, also called Elizabeth Greenly (her father's sister), who was married to her cousin Edward Greenly. Edward was the King's Proctor (Head Lawyer), and through Edward's associations, Eliza would often meet with members of the Royal Family.

From my Uncle and Aunt Greenly. Norbiton Hall, Kingston in Surrey. (1784).

Though you are too far from the Metropolis to be infected by the balloon fever, yet you cannot be unacquainted with the fame of Lunardi who has communicated this disease to London and its environs. On Wednesday last he set out on his aerial voyage in a balloon of nearly twice the size of the Octagon Chapel at Bath, accompanied only by a dog and a cat, for the balloon would not admit the English gentleman who designed going with him.

He went to a considerable height, where he experienced intense cold and descended at the end of 3 hours, almost frozen and covered with icicles. He went about thirty miles and landed in Hertfordshire, in doing which he would have met with some difficulty, had it not been for a woman who assisted him. Some men, her companions, ran away frightened. The concourse of people assembled to see Lunardi take his flight was immense; among the number was my mother, who went with a friend as curious as herself; she was much delighted and escaped without having her pocket picked, for which she was indebted to a man with a drawn sword who protected her.

The balloon was seen from hence and moved very steadily. Everybody is interested in Mr. Lunardi, who is a very ingenious young man, secretary to the Neapolitan Ambassador. Another experiment of the kind will be made a week hence by Mr. Blanchard, who hopes to be the first person to cross the English Channel and land in France.

These successful trials make me hope that in a short time Balloons will be the general mode of conveyance; distances will be nothing, roads of no consequence and highwaymen and footpads not to be feared. Fortunate would it be for this neighbourhood could they soar above them now but alas these ladies who are seduced to go abroad at night run a great risk, indeed so many robberies have been committed that few have the courage to quit their own houses of an evening.

October 1st 1787. From my Uncle Goodison. The 'Minuet' I have sent you was composed by Handel when he was quite a child and could hardly write his notes. I have the original manuscript.

February 16th 1789. We were at our other house in Abergavenny, in Monk Street (the house was left to us by my Grandmother upon her death). The whole town was illuminated on account of the King's recovery from his long & melancholy illness. The houses and villages around were all illuminated on this occasion and even the poorest cottage window had its farthing candles to twinkle forth an assurance of the loyalty of those within.

The mobs smash the windows of any house that does not illuminate.

From London, May 24th 1791. A letter from Eliza to her grandmother. I have my first lesson in oil painting of Mr. Abraham Pether who is a delightful man, with a great deal of genius, not only in painting but in music and other sciences, having constructed two curious telescopes and an electrical machine.

On May 28th 1791. We have been to Warren Hastings's trial at Westminster Hall. Mr. Furye, gave us tickets to the Duke of Newcastle's box, entered through the Exchequer's office. Hastings is accused of corruption in his office while serving in India. Some are saying the trial is more a debate between two opposed visions of empire; the one represented by Hastings, based on ideas of absolute power and conquest in pursuit of the exclusive national interests of the colonizer, versus one represented by Edmund Burke, of sovereignty based on a recognition of the rights of the colonies themselves. My father and mother were pleased with the vivacity of Burke's speech.
The Judges afforded me some amusement, posing on the Woolsacks in their huge wigs, they put me in mind of Gloucestershire sheep lying on a sunny bank.

May 26th 1792. I went to see some of Gainsborough's paintings which are exhibiting for sale. For one cottage scene four hundred and fifty guineas are asked. A pair – one of two children in a cottage, and behind the children, a fine tabby cat, and, thro' the closed casement, a robin on a snowy spray is looking on. The companion piece has only one child and a cat, but for the pair is six hundred guineas demanded.

June 9th 1792. We went to Bradberry's Exhibition in Bond Street of optical deceptions which he calls 'practical magic'. Many curious effects are produced by reflecting mirrors, so placed a bring the object they reflect in such relief as to seem standing in space. A likeness of the King and of an old lady who you think you could take by the hand. On looking into a mirror on the top of a box against the wall you see the figure of a gentleman who presents you with a bouquet, you attempt to take it, but your fingers meet in air, the flowers are withdrawn, and a naked dagger is presented to your heart.

From Mrs. Stokes, Barmouth on the Welsh Coast, August 1st 1793. This country is unspeakably beautiful, all the way from Welsh Pool I never before saw such a mixture of the soft and the sublime. The mountains are adorned with verdure and lovely vales and the wildest of them are devoid of those savage horrors that characterise the Peak of Derbyshire. The appearance and manners of the inhabitants are very interesting. They are free from the insolence or servility of the common people of most parts of England. They salute travellers in a manner so benevolent and cordial as to remind us forcibly of our descent from one common parent. The women in general are handsome, the children healthy and clean. This is the finest beach for bathing I ever saw and precludes all fear from the most timid bather.

Abergavenny, September 5th 1793. We reached Stroud and went to see Mr. Cook's manufactory of woollen cloth. We were shown the carding machine, the spinning Billys and spinning Jennys, the burling and teazling, the beating and shearing the cloths.

London, May 10th 1794. I am sitting with the artist Inglehart for my miniature. He has painted Lady Oxford. Friday, we called on her. I was much pleased with her appearance – she has a sweet and good-tempered countenance. Her mother, Mrs. Scott, looks a vulgar managing woman.

London, May 24th 1794. It is imagined that many who are sent to the Tower will be found guilty of High Treason, as the warrant (of which seventy have been issued), charges them with that crime. I see "God save the King" written on the walls more frequently than "No war" or "Charles Fox for ever". Some democratic gentlemen have said within my hearing, that they commiserated with the French having been, forced by us and our Allies, to murder the French King Louis and his Queen, Marie Antoinette.

London, June 14th 1794. By Colonel Smith's kindness we saw Mr. Townley's collection of antique marbles. He called the bust of Clitea his 'mistress'. On one night the illuminations for Lord Howe's victory, Lord Stanhope, refusing to have lights, had all his windows broken. Lord Stanhope made his exit by a back door and has not been to town since. The second night we made a circuit of five miles to see all the various squares. The crowd were orderly; but there were guns, squibs, crackers, and rockets.

Titley Court, January 1795. The cold was so intense in January and to the 9th of February that often, early in the morning, the ink froze in my pen. When the thaw came on the 9th February there was a tremendous flood. The water was four feet deep in the stables. Rats were driven into the trees. At Hereford, the scene was dreadful and Mrs. Bodeham and the Brewsters heard at their houses the roaring river, and the cries of the terrified people, on the night of the 10th.

Titley Court, March 24th 1795. I had a letter from Mr. Abraham Pether to inform me that he had sent a landscape that I had painted, a view of Bredwardine Bridge, to the Exhibition at Somerset House.

Summer, 1795. We made a small tour. Bath, June 5th 1795. Among others that are here is my old dancing mistress Miss Fleming who was delighted to see me; she has twice been to Paris; at the beginning of the French revolution, she went with the American Ambassador to the Bastille the day after it was taken and threw down some stones from the top of the walls. She brought away as relics two rusty keys, picked up in the archives room, and a ladle from the Governor's kitchen. Her second visit was not so prosperous, she was once very near being shot & narrowly escaped being taken for a spy. By the last accounts from Paris such rapid strides is famine making that people drop down daily in the streets & women throw their children into the river and leap in after them.

My most interesting hours in Bath were spent with Mrs. & Miss Harriet Bowlder; they made a tour three years ago of eight hundred miles, and visited the intimate friends of the latter, namely Lady Eleanor Butler and Miss Ponsonby, at Llangollen. Miss H.B has taken views of the scenery around, and of their pretty cottage, in a little book which has its leaves bordered round and ornamented in the most elegant manner by Miss. Ponsonby, who writes a beautiful hand. Miss H.B. has executed some very clever landscapes in crayons, and paints transparencies in a peculiar style of her own. Miss H.B and her brother published the works of Shakespere with all references that might offend removed. There are those who are saying that to 'Bowdlerize' is to soften a work to remove offence – either religious, political or of an intimate nature.

A warehouse has opened here of the Derby manufactory. I never saw China so beautiful, but the price is very high. Cups and saucers richly painted are a guinea and a half each. A set of Tea China, a yellow ground with medallions of Derbyshire views, twenty guineas. The Prince of Wales has ordered a dinner set that is to cost two hundred pounds. I am very sorry to hear that his marriage is already supposed to be an unhappy one; his temper is altered, and he is continually drinking cherry brandy to intoxication.

Clifton Hill near Bristol, June 13th 1795. We had a wedding next door last Friday, Mr. Phillip Miles to Miss Whetham, daughter of an Irish Dean. He is the son of Alderman Miles who is worth four hundred thousand pounds: he give his son one hundred thousand pounds and would have given him double had he married more to his approbation. The lady is handsome, but I fancy has no other motive than the gentleman's purse for uniting herself to him. It is said she calls him her 'Golden Calf'.

Our friend Mrs. Waddington is here to consult Doctor Beddoes and is trying the effect of inhaling his Oxygen Gas.

London, May 2nd 1796. We reached London in the evening. Thanks to the coach boy of our chariot and Philips' broad back effectively hiding the horses, my mother has been so courageous that she forgot to make her usual anxious enquiries of the Innkeeper and Postillions whether the horses were 'quiet.'

Mrs Shepherd told us a pleasing anecdote of our good King. Old Macklin who is ninety-seven years old goes frequently to the Theatre and always sits in the pit near the stage, that he may hear the better. He was pointed out to His Majesty who immediately made him a bow. This public mark of Royal notice was highly gratifying to the old man. Another instance of the King's good feelings occurred lately at the Opera House. It is usual when the Royal family are there, for the dancers of the conclusion of the Ballet to remain in their last attitude till the King's departure. But when present a few evenings ago, the Green Curtain fell the moment the dance was ended. It was done by the King's orders, the stage being very cold and many of the dancers had suffered extremely from standing still after their violent exertions.

London, July 27th 1797. You will be surprised to see Colonel Capper out of powder, not that he does not pay the powder tax, but because it saves time and trouble and renders him independent of his valet. When in London he queues and powders like the rest of the loyal world.

From my cousin, Miss Greenly. Weymouth, September 16th 1799. We are very intimate with Miss. Planta, English reader and factotum to all the ladies of the Royal family. She related the dreadful circumstance of Princess Elizabeth's favourite dog falling from the top of the house. 'Time' was taken up for dead, and a surgeon recommended a vein in his neck should be opened. My Mother, however, suggested her Embrocation of Rum and Castile soap and gave some of it to Miss Planta. It effected wonders and 'Time' was perfectly cured.

A few days afterwards Princess Elizabeth called, saying, "Mrs. Greenly, I am infinitely obliged to you for curing my dog and I shall send him to return thanks". This she did, and the favourite showed his gratitude by gnawing on a chicken bone. Honours were pressed upon my mother.

The King asked her how she did, whether she bathed in the sea, where she lived, and the Queen bade the little Princess Charlotte make a curtsey to Mrs. Greenly. His Majesty has since talked familiarly to her on the subject of the weather. I fancy he may have been told of her extreme attachment to him and he kindly observed her loyalty.

Bombay, January 13th 1800. From Mrs. Deere. I think the human species here much inferior to those at home. In point of intellect, they are much below standard. I was delighted with Rio de Janeiro, but it is inhabited by a sad and inferior race, a mixture of Portuguese and Africans.

Titley Court, July 1800. We have had eleven weeks of uninterrupted dry weather, unknown in England for over forty years. In Radnor Forest, owning to a furze fire, the peat was burning to a depth of from eight to ten feet and was only put out by the heavy rain at the end of August.

Titley Court, 1802. On Tuesday February 16th 1802, Captain Mathew Flinders, sailed His Majesty's ship, 'The Investigator', and discovered the southern coast of Australia. He later named an island, lakes, bays, and mountains after Lady Elizabeth Greenly, wife of Admiral Sir Isaac Coffin Greenly.

Titley Church, Herefordshire. April 4th 1811. Eliza married Admiral Sir Isaac Coffin, who took the name Greenly after. The marriage was at eight o'clock in the morning at Titley Church. The wedding party returned to Titley Court after the ceremony and had a wedding breakfast there. Afterwards, Sir Isaac and Lady Greenly set out for London.

Elizabeth wrote a number of letters to her parents while she was away with Sir Isaac for the first time as a married woman.

London, April 6th 1811. Sir Isaac took me immediately to call on his sister Mrs Barwell, who had a house in Montague Square. I thought her the most beautiful woman I had ever seen.

Weymouth, Dorset May 7th 1811. We took up at my cousins' Greenly, at Monte Video. On the 9th Sir Isaac set out for London to attend the Prince Regent's fete at Carlton House. I remained with my cousins till the 14th when I came to Bath and took up my abode at The Elephant and Castle Hotel.

Titley Court, May 19th 1811. From my mother. We had a dreadful journey home, arriving through thunder and lightning and violent rain. The hailstones were so large and fell so thick, it was quite terrifying. We had upwards of eighty panes of glass broke, not a window in front of the house escaped. Two men at Eardisland were killed by the electric fluid. When Mrs. Brown of the Cat and Fiddle Tavern heard of your marriage she said, "the best thing in the county is gone out of it".

Portsmouth, May 26th 1811. At Portsmouth everyone knows Sir Isaac. I am rather an object of curiosity & I hear that I am guessed to be under twenty years old & that people wonder why the Admiral should have married so young a wife. We went to see the process of tarring ropes, and baking biscuits, and called at the Naval College. Sir Isaac told the naval students, who were as young as thirteen years old, that their post as midship men was to ensure the total subordination of the common sailors. He told them that they were superior and could therefore treat the sailors as they wished and could call for any of them to be punished if they disobeyed their orders or were reluctant or surly with them. I did not like to hear this.

London, July 20th 1811. I dined at four o'clock at Mrs. Barwell's, and at six o'clock I began my toilette. At seven o'clock, Mrs. Furye joined us. Mrs. Barwell dressed my head. I had the diamond sprig in front, a line of small stones on one side and three very large ones on the other. A bunch of curls hid my cropped pate behind. On the way to the Palace, I was much amused by a respectable looking man, reading the motto under our coat of arms, and being much puzzled by "Fal Y Gallo".

Sir Isaac named me to the Prince Regent, and I was honoured with a very polite bow. The Duke of Clarence told me he hoped I found Sir Isaac a good husband. The other Royal Dukes all spoke to Sir Isaac and politely noticed me.

The Duchesse d'angoulême wore the pearls which belonged to her unfortunate mother, and were saved in so extra-ordinary a manner, during her imprisonment. She was the eldest child of the French King Louis XVI and Marie Antoinette, and the only one of their offspring to survive the French Revolution. She was imprisoned in the Temple, the remains of a medieval fortress in Paris, from August 1792 to December 1795, on the eve of her seventeenth birthday. During this time, her parents were guillotined and her younger brother – imprisoned in a separate room and cruelly neglected – died of illness.

Titley Court, July 1811. The whole month passed in hay making, visiting, and being visited by our neighbours.

Titley Court, July 31st 1811. Mr. James Watt (of steam engine fame and fortune) came from Birmingham unexpectedly, to dine with us. Eliza noted, "He gave an interesting account of the atrocities he saw in Paris at the start of the French Revolution. I never heard anything so horrible!"

Titley Court, August 11th 1811. There is a comet visible by the naked eye. Visible for several nights.

Titley Court, October 7th 1811. Mr. Ferriday dined with us. From being employed in the iron business at three pennies a day, he has become the greatest ironmaster in the Kingdom. He has fifty thousand workmen to whom he pays five thousand guineas weekly and burns five thousand tons of coal. I was introduced also to Mr. and Mrs. Josiah Wedgwood, of the pottery fame, who also came to dine.

Everton near Liverpool, October 7th 1811. Went to Mr. William Earls of Everton, near Liverpool. October 9th, rode to Liverpool to see the docks.

Everton near Liverpool, October 14th 1811. We drove to Liverpool once more which is about three miles long and said to contain near one hundred thousand inhabitants. It abounds with fine public buildings and spacious docks full of vessels. The quarry from which the new docks have been built is perhaps the most extensive in England; it is a yellow freestone; blocks of immense size are cut from it and large enough to form prodigious columns without a joint. On the top of the hill, where the quarry lies, is a public walk commanding a panoramic view of the town and river Mersey, covered with vessels. The Cheshire coast opposite and Denbigh and Flintshire mountains beyond.

Liverpool, being new built, is far more regular than country towns in general. There are about one thousand ships in the various docks, a sign of the stagnation in trade.

Spekelands near Liverpool, October 21st 1811. On Friday we drove to Liverpool to see Mr. Earle's oil mills. They are worked by a steam engine of fifty horsepower. We saw the processes of cleaning the mustard and rape seed, the grinding of which is accomplished in a mill like a cyder mill, but with two large stones instead of one.

Llantrisant in Wales, December 29th 1811. Lord Hood, who is a very fine old gentleman of eighty-eight years old, and speaking as he does through his nose said, "You are a lucky fellow Coffin, Everybody speaks well of Lady Greenly". Sir Isaac replied, "And nobody speaks well of me, my Lord?". "I did not say *that*", replied Lord Hood abruptly.

July 4th 1812. Sir Isaac and I came early to Llanidloes in Wales, where he got into a coach to go northwards, and I proceeded to Titley. I felt much at parting from Sir Isaac, though I little dreamed of the cruel part he was about to act, and that I was not to see him again for seven years!

At this time, I was much engaged in writing my first volume of Practical Sermons for every day in a year, which greatly contributed to soothe my mind and draw it from painful thoughts.

Plymouth Dock, May 8th 1812. At Falmouth we could see from the Inn, a packet arrived from Lisbon, and another from Malta, and boats full of fish – cods, pollacks, and haddocks as large as a man.

Penzance, May 14th 1812. The blocks of granite ("Moor Stones") that we saw hewing, were for the new bridge over the river Thames in London. The Cornish language was generally spoken through the County as late as 1640. It is now quite extinct, the last person who could speak it, was a woman at St. Pauls, who died some years ago.

Portledge Estate, Devon 1812. This is the spot that the Coffins settled at when they came over with William the Conqueror. The parish of Alwington, and the surrounding area, was given to the family by William the Conqueror, as part of a reward for loyalty and service during the Norman Conquest.

It is now inhabited by Mr. Pyne Coffin, whose father lives at Bath. Mrs. Coffin was at home and allowed us to go over the Mansion. The oak staircase and many of the chimney pieces are very richly carved and the Coffin arms, exactly the same as Sir Isaacs, are emblazoned in many places.

Titley Court, December 1812. Lord Byron was again at nearby Eywood Manor, to visit the beautiful Lady Oxford. His countenance was not to me a pleasing one. I never felt easy in his company. His eye gave me more the idea of "the poets in a fine frenzy rolling", than any I ever beheld, but it had no soft and gentle expression.

Titley Court, January 13th 1812. There was a general thanksgiving for the victories of the allied armies on the Continent. So much snow is falling and is seventeen feet deep in places.

London, May 10th 1814. I took lessons in oil painting as usual of Laporte & sat for my Portrait with his daughter.

London, June 5th 1814. Went to see a painting of Shakespeare in an engraver's shop in Great Newport Street. It was found in a pawnbroker's shop and is on panel, and painted on an absorbent ground and has every mark of originality.

June 28th 1814. An account came of Wellington's victory against Napoleon Bonaparte, afterwards called the Battle of Waterloo.

July 14th 1814. There was a general thanksgiving on account of the peace. My mother had a calf killed and distributed the meat among the poor of Titley.

November 27th 1814. My forty fourth birthday. Susan played the piano while our servants danced in the Hall. My mother gave her dinner of meat and pudding to my school children, forty-six in number.

Cowbridge, November 28th 1814. Last night Mr. W. Nicholl amused us with a very good microscope, lately given him by his sister at a cost of twenty-seven guineas. An insect which chanced to be in the water decanter and was not larger than a full-grown mite, became five inches long and a very extraordinary personage he appeared.

Boulogne sur mer, France. February 22nd om1815. I find the people here very different. We are settled in Bonaparte's country house, two miles from Boulogne, now inhabited by Madame Clocheville; my bedroom is the one of the Hero (as he is called here) had occupied and the bed is the same.

Titley Court, August 18th 1815. Poor Mr. Thomas King was found drowned in the river Arrow, close to his house at the nearby cottages at Noke. He went out leaving the candles burning in his sitting room and never returned. On letting out the river mill pond, in the morning, his body was found sticking upright in the mud.

Titley Court, February 8th 1816. Little Robert Mundy is a sweet and interesting child, but alas! He is given a great deal too much medicine. Norman, the family apothecary from Ilkeston, actually wanted to bleed the poor little fellow, merely because he had a slight cough, but his sister would not let him. Like most country apothecaries, Norman bleeds without mercy.

Titley Court, February 15th 1817. Completed the building of Rhiwlas Cottage. I built it for John Evans, who was our coachman, one of the best and most active we ever had. But his wife was a Londoner, and soon prevailed on her husband to leave us and the country, and to settle in a shop in a confined alley in the Metropolis.

Titley Court, June 8th 1817. A busy week as the workmen put up a 'Water Closet' in what had been a cupboard for china in the Chintz room.

Titley Court, December 2nd 1818. An old Scotch soldier who at the age of one hundred and one years old, was walking up to London by desire of the Prince Regent. He had applied for the renewal of a Pension he had forfeited by serving in America, where he had fought for the Americans in their war of independence from their English rulers. The Prince sent word that if he would come up to London, he would give him his Christmas Box; his Pension will doubtless be restored. His name is William Johnson, and he had served at the Battle of Minden in 1759 with the English army that time.

Titley Court, September 17th 1819. While we were at breakfast a Chase drove up to the door, and to our great astonishment it contained Sir Isaac. He insisted on seeing me. I went to him in the drawing room; much agitating conversation took place, but on his repeated assurances that he was sorry he had deserted me & now wished to make reparation, I entreated my parents to receive him and forget the past, which they most kindly consented to, for my sake.

Brighton, November 22nd 1819. At Sir John Shelley's we met the Duke of Wellington, who had defeated Napoleon at the Battle of Waterloo in 1814. His Grace was very pleasant and good humoured & enjoyed partridge shooting as much as any schoolboy, and with about as much effect.

London, September 6th 1819. A mob at night filled St. James's Square, surrounding Lord Castlereagh's house; six Horse Guards kept them quiet but when I came home, I found our windows in Coventry Street broke.

London, September 7th 1819. A large eclipse of the Sun.

London, June 20th 1820. Mrs. Caskell called to take me to Newgate. I was charmed with Mrs. Elizabeth Fry, who escorted us everywhere; she had bought order out of chaos. Mrs. Fry & another very respectable Quaker, told us that of all the wretched females bought to the prison, hardly any had had religious education and most of them could not read. I have never heard anything more impressive than Mrs. Fry's manner of reading the Bible and commenting upon it. She has two reading schools, one for adults, and the other for the children of the prisoners. All the needlework done by the latter, is sold for their benefit.

London, April 11th 1823. We went from Salisbury Cathedral, where we visited John Greenly, and travelled in a Chase to Stonehenge, which surpasses all the ideas I had of it. I chipped off some bits from one of the stones, with a large flint that I picked up, and took them to the garden in Titley Court.

Clifton, Bristol. March 19th 1825. We went to see a collection of wild beasts belonging to Wombwell. Among them three cubs, the progeny of a tigress and a male lion. They played like kittens and were about a foot high.

Titley Court, July 1st 1825. Mrs. Mynors showed me in Coke's Reports, an entry for "Greneleye's Case", which was settled in 1610. The case concerning a dispute between Phillipe, Stephen, and Owen Greneleye, of some land in Staunton-on-Arrow. Those lands are now owned by me as part of the Titley Estate.

Bath, February 9th 1825. We went to a lecture on the application of steam engines to machinery; the models were beautiful and worked to perfection. We had one of Mr. Watt's engines and one of Mr. Trevigthick's, more simple but less safe. There was a pretty little model of a Carriage moved by steam along a railway as now used at Leeds for bringing coal to town and invented by a Mr. Blenkinsop; it brings sixty tons of coal and travels three miles an hour.

Titley Court, January 14th 1826. Cousin Louisa Hastings and I went to see Mary Goodwin, said to be one hundred and seven years old; she was very deaf, her eyesight imperfect, she complained of pain and watchfulness; I remembered her as a gossiping old woman, she was the Midwife of the neighbourhood.

In March, Bodenham's Bank at Hereford, the old Bank at Ludlow, and the Leominster Bank all stopped payment.

In July, Mr. Mynor's waggoner, ploughing in the field close to Enjobb, turned up a large broad Gold Ring, having this motto neatly cut in the inside; 'KEPE FAYTH TIL DEATH.' Mr. M supposes it to have belonged to some of the adherents of Charles II. A spot near Beggars Bush is still called Rails Yatt, a corruption from Royal Yatt, the Royal Gate through which the King passed. Tradition relates that he named the place called the Bush, as 'Beggars Bush' because he said, "I am a beggar & wanderer".

Bath, February 28th 1829. We visited Lord Nelson's flagship 'HMS Victory'. We went all over it and down to the cockpit and the small room adjoining, in which Nelson died. A cousin, Reverend John Greenly, served with Lord Nelson at the Battle of Trafalgar in 1805, and now lives at Salisbury Cathedral, where he is a member of the clergy of The Close. John has letters, written by his own hand at the time, and these give the words of Nelson, describing his famous signal before the battle, and also of his dying words. These words will forever be etched in the hearts and minds of all Englishmen.

Titley Court, January 27th 1830. The poor blind woman, Sarah Griffiths, who for many years, since I was fourteen or fifteen years old, I had maintained, died after keeping her bed for near two years. She learned to spin and could in many ways assist herself. She was truly pious, patient under almost constant suffering. I sent to the funeral some of our servants and Louisa sent some of hers; my schoolmaster Bradley attended with six boys to sing with the Procession.

Titley Court, February 25th 1830. I began to dig the foundation of a new stone cottage at Bircher, the old timber one built by my great-great grandfather Andrew Greenly, being in a complete state of decay. He built it on the want of an old servant.

Titley Court, March 7th 1833. A mad dog came across our village; it bit several pigs which were obliged to be killed; it also bit the nose of a fine young heifer of ours. The wound was cauterised, but it was too late. Our man, Richard Joseph, shot the dog at the turning ways, just outside the village. On the 18th March, our heifer died of Hydrophobia. The heifer, at the end, took on the same savagery as the dog. Thank God that no villagers were bitten as hydrophobia in a man is a truly dreadful sight. We do not know from where the dog came or what caused its madness.

Titley Church, January 7th 1834. A very sad day. My dear father William Greenly died. He died peacefully in his own bed, in his beloved Titley Court. He was carried to the church by eleven poor men, who had grey coats & black breeches given to them, and hatbands and gloves. Our men servants were in mourning cloaks and crape hatbands. Nine tenants were also in mourning, and all very handsome and respectable without parade. On the 19th the whole family went to Titley Church, which was hung with black.

The next month, on the 10th February, I began the building of the Vault at the end of the church, into which I intend my dear father's remains should be removed to. Later, I had a monument made with the following words:

Beneath the tower at the west end of this church lie the remains of William GREENLY of Titley Court in the county of Hereford, whose uprightness as a Magistrate and kindness as a friend and a neighbour and piety and benevolence as a Christian during the course of his long life endeared him to all who knew him. He died January 7th, 1834, aged 93.

Later, after Eliza's death, the monument would include words in memory of her mother, who outlived Eliza by a few years:

Also, in the same vault lies the remains of Elizabeth relict of the above William GREENLY. She was born April 15th, 1751, and died February 8th, 1843, in the 92nd year of her age.

Titley Court, April 30th 1834. I found my mother was agitated by a letter from a London attorney at law, at Sir Isaac's desire. The letter was demanding of her, as my dear father's executrix, the payment of all of the arrears of my four hundred pounds a year ever since 1811! I replied, as I had done to former ones, that no arrears were due, as the four hundred pounds had been regularly paid to me, Sir Isaac's wife, by consent given under his own hand. My father, who was a lawyer himself, had insisted that this contract was made to protect my inheritance.

Titley Court, October 4th 1834. Major Coffin, when here, was very urgent with me to grant Sir Isaac an interview: He added that he could not defend his uncle, he could only lament that he was not like any other human being. I felt it my duty as a Christian to comply and write to say I would spend a day at Cheltenham. We went to the Clarence Hotel where we found Sir Isaac in bed; he expressed himself very glad to see me and thanked me for coming. Mrs. Guy Coffin says that my visit has done him much good: in high spirits and with long stories he is just what he was. As to my placing any confidence in Sir Isaac, that is nonsense, but my mind is far more comfortable with the idea of being at peace instead of war, but having been twice deceived, I can feel no certainty. In a month's time he

THE GREENLYS: HISTORICAL EYEWITNESSES 1415 - 1865

may change again.

When I was visiting him, I could not help smiling to myself at some of Sir Isaac's awkward attempts to account for his unkind proceedings. Among others he assured me that it was King George IV's particular orders that he dropped the name of Greenly (a likely story!), and then he proceeded to hint that when he was in actual possession of my property, he would have no objection to resume it!

Titley Court, November 19th 1834. Poor old Nelly Price of the Shawl, just up the road from Titley, breathed her last at the age of one hundred and six years old. Her family, called 'Preece' in older times, had been resident around Titley for many generations.

Titley Court, 1836. In 1836 the 'Tithe Commutation Act' was passed in parliament, following years of grumbling by farmers who have to pay one tenth ('tithe' means a tenth) of their produce to support the church. The Act allows for a money payment rather than a produce payment. In order for the church to work out who should pay what tithe, commissioners collected information on every field subject to tithe in England. The church needed to know who owned the field, who was the tenant, what was grown, what it was worth and what the tithe money payment amounted to. Huge 'Tithe Barns' were built to hold the crops until they could be sold on behalf of the church. A farmer could choose to pay in crops, which were collected and taken to the tithe barn, or pay the local clergy with money instead. The church was very wealthy. Even small parishes would have a large Vicarage next door to the church, where the Vicar would live and entertain guests. The parish, in addition to the tithe, would also provide the local clergyman with a few acres that he would rent out.

Accompanying this information was 'The Apportionment', which was a large map. Eliza viewed the map for North Herefordshire and confirmed that it represented the many lands held by her and by her cousins, John Senior, John Junior, Thomas and Mary Greenly. John Senior was the father of Richard Greenly. John Junior was Richard's brother.

Eliza noted the entries for the fields and woodland at Woodhalehill, in Staunton-on-Arrow. John Greneleye was Eliza and Richard's common ancestor and was granted the manor of Woodhalehill by King Henry VIII in 1525. From that place, John would also acquire lands in neighbouring Titley, and settle the family at Titley Court; the birthplace of Eliza and her home until her death.

Titley Court, January 29th 1839. Eliza died. She was sixty-six years old. Her father was ninety-three years old when he died and her mother, who survived Eliza by four years, was ninety-three years old when she died. Sir Isaac also died in 1839. Her mother had a monument made for Titley Church. The wording is below:

Sacred to the memory of the Lady Elizabeth Brown Coffin GREENLY, only child of the late William GREENLY esq. of Titley Court and of Elizabeth his wife; and wife of Admiral Sir Isaac COFFIN Bart G.C.H. who took the name of GREENLY by letters patent on his marriage. She was born on the 27th of November 1771 and died on the 29th of January 1839 aged 67. This monument is erected by her surviving parent in memory of her virtues and of her talents which she dedicated through life to the cause of religion and morality. In her character were blended the qualities most loved of God - Piety, Humility and Sincerity joined to a clear understanding and matchless sweetness of disposition. Her resignation and cheerfulness under severe and protracted trials attested the firmness of her faith in "him who was made perfect through suffering" and inspired the tenderest affection in those around her and the deepest sorrow at her loss. Her remains rest in the vault underneath the tower erected by herself at the west end of this church.

After the death of Eliza's mother Elizabeth, ownership of Titley Court and the Greenly estate and rents, went first to Eliza's cousin and dear friend Louisa Hastings, wife of Sir Thomas Hastings. They had been living at the Parsonage in Titley, just down the hill from Titley Court. Then ownership passed to another cousin, Charles Williams Allen, who inherited all, and took the name Greenly.

Once again, Eliza was acting to ensure that her beloved 'Greenly' family name, and all of its past, and future history, would never be lost or forgotten.

ABOUT THE AUTHOR

David Greenly has researched the Greenly family history for more than 30 years. Ever keen to share his research, the author created a family history website (greenlyhistory.com) ten years ago, but had always wanted to share some of the history in the form of a book, where, hopefully readers can transport themselves back into the shoes of a few distant relatives and walk alongside them, and share in their fascinating stories from the past.

I do hope you enjoyed the journey!

Printed in Great Britain
by Amazon